THE NIGHT BEFORE

JACINTA HOWARD

Copyright © 2017 by Jacinta Howard

All rights reserved.

No part of this book may be reproduced in any form or by any electronic or mechanical means, including information storage and retrieval systems, without written permission from the author, except for the use of brief quotations in a book review.

Edited By: Little Pear Editing

ONE

Ava scanned the crowded living room, releasing a soft sigh as she twirled her candy cane in her rum and coke. Her eyes flitted from the half-drunk guy in the corner of the room who was vying for the attention of a woman who looked as bored as she was, to a woman dressed in a seductive elf costume, as if it were Halloween, before landing on her friend. Ellie looked up and Ava raised her brows.

"Ten more minutes," Ellie mouthed, barely able to look away from the tall guy she was hugged up with.

Ava sighed and plastered a fake smile on her face. For the tenth time in the past hour and a half, she wondered why she'd let Ellie drag her to this party. On the occasions that she returned home, she preferred to spend them hanging out with her mom. Ava didn't get to see her nearly as often as she would've liked.

But instead of hanging with her mom, watching bad Christmas movies on Lifetime and drinking too much rum and coke, she was out at this soul-sucking party with her best friend from high school. She didn't even remember half of these people, and didn't want to. High school—the entire town— was a dead-end waste of space. As soon as Ava graduated, she'd left. She didn't even wait out the summer before heading to college.

The longer she sat on the plush oversized couch that seemed to be made for sleeping, not entertaining, the more convinced she was that the life was literally being zapped out of her. She pulled out her phone and glanced at it. She'd give Ellie *five* more minutes and then she was kicking rocks. She clicked on her Kindle app and started reading.

"You know reading at a party is pretty rude."

"Excuse me?" Ava lifted her eyes from her phone, her brow furrowed at the owner of the deep baritone who'd interrupted her, just as she was getting to the good part. Her gaze settled on a tall figure, hovering over her.

"Reading at a party. It's rude. But then you were stuck up in high school, so I'm not surprised."

Ava's mouth parted slightly.

"Excuse me?"

Who the heck did this guy think he was? She craned her neck looking up at him, trying to make out his admittedly handsome features. His skin was the color of dark roast coffee, just before the cream and his eyes were aware but lively with playful intrigue. His beard was groomed but still managed to give him a rugged edge, and he was wearing a dark blue sweater that stretched snuggly across his chest. She was drawing a blank, though she didn't know how that was possible. If this dude had gone to school with her, there was *no way* she would've forgotten him. He was still smiling cockily at her and she frowned. Fine or not, he was an asshole.

"I was *not* stuck up," she muttered, internally kicking herself for not thinking of a better comeback.

"Yes, you were," he refuted, still grinning when she

frowned. "You used to walk the hallways with your nose so far up in the air, it's a wonder it didn't get stuck there."

He seated himself next to her on the plush couch, stretching his long legs out comfortably and crossing his booted feet at the ankles.

"What are you reading? It must be damn enthralling."

Ava stared at him, shocked by his audacity.

"Excuse me?"

"You already said that, Ava. Twice."

He flashed another overly-confident grin her way and she tilted her head, glaring at him. The way he said her name was familiar, as if he'd been saying it forever, and it was doing weird things to her stomach. He was still peering nosily at her phone. She snatched it from his gaze and his lips curled up, revealing a smile that probably typically worked to leave women dumb and panty-less. But she wasn't typical. Or dumb.

"I'll bet it's some feminist shit, huh? Roxanne Gay? Chimamanda Ngozi Adichie? bell hooks?"

He arched a brow, patiently waiting for her to answer.

"First of all, you may *think* you know me but I don't have any idea who you are and don't really care to. And I don't appreciate you inviting yourself into my personal space and then interrupting my reading just to insult me." Ava's voice raised slightly, and she sat forward, pointing a finger at his muscled chest.

His smiled widened and Ava felt her entire body heat. "You're still just as cute as you were in high school."

She blinked caught off guard.

"Nah, never mind," he said, his deep voice dropping an octave. His gaze roamed over her features, taking in her curly twist-out, long eyelashes, and lips she'd painted coral pink. "You're even more beautiful now."

He was switching gears fast and she frowned. Why wasn't her brain keeping up with him? She did this for a living. She was known for her quick wit and ability to persuade, qualities that helped her immensely as a network publicist. She wasn't easily charmed by anyone. *She* did the charming.

"I'm Elias Young, by the way."

"I would say it's nice to you meet you, but it hasn't been thus far."

He chuckled, his eyes dancing with amusement. "Now that was just mean, Ava."

"Are your feelings hurt?"

"A little bit, yes."

She arched a brow, holding back a smile at his deliberately crestfallen expression. There was nothing cute about a grown ass man pouting. But damn if this dude didn't make it *sexy*.

"You should learn how to talk to people if you're gonna act all sensitive when they call you on your bullshit, Elias."

He laughed, his eyes telling her he was thoroughly enjoying their exchange. "Kendrick is my cousin," he offered unexpectedly, bobbing his head toward the host of this dead party, who was now whispering in Ellie's ear. "I went to East too but I was a few years older than you. Obviously, we ran in different circles."

"Obviously."

He chuckled again at the disdain in her tone, a deep sound that made her pulse start beating too hard. She frowned again, thrown by her reaction to him.

"What were you reading?" He shifted his position on the couch, getting even more comfortable. Clearly, he wasn't leaving. And there was no way she was letting some fine, strange man run her off from the only acceptable seating in the house.

"*The Road*," she finally answered, just as "Baby It's Cold Outside" came on.

"*The Road?*" he echoed incredulously. "At a *Christmas Eve party*, Ava? That's gotta be one of the bleakest books ever written."

She chuckled reluctantly, looking off toward the middle of the living room, where a few couples had started dancing.

"It is pretty depressing," she conceded. "But it's poetic."

"*Borrowed time and borrowed world and borrowed eyes with which to sorrow it,*" he said, quoting a line from the book.

Her gaze met his, and her mouth fell open, but only a little. *Who was this dude?* He smiled, watching as she hastily took another sip of her drink, hoping to cover her reaction.

"I guarantee someone is writing that on a suicide note right now."

She laughed before she could stop herself, shaking her head at him.

"So, do you still live here, Elias?"

He bit the corner of his lip, an almost satisfied glint entering his dark brown eyes.

"Nope. I'm back visiting my folks for the holiday." Subconsciously, her eyes took in his ring finger. He wasn't wearing one. He noticed her checking him out and his smile became more relaxed. Damn his fine ass. "I work in Atlanta."

"What do you do?"

"Ah, come on," he groaned, throwing his head back. "Don't tell me you're one of those." He lowered his voice tilting his head as he studied her.

"One of *what*?" She arched a brow.

"One of those women who judges dudes based on their occupation."

"You got all of that from me asking what you do for a living? That's kinda presumptuous. And also kinda sexist."

He grinned, eyeing her. "I'm not sexist. I love women. Everything about them." His voice had dipped an octave, his gaze roaming slowly over her. He grinned lazily and she shifted in her seat, her heart beating way too fast. "I also abhor America's patriarchal power structure and the objectification of women in the realm of American pop culture and society at large."

She rolled her eyes, holding in another smile. He chuckled.

"All I'm sayin' is my gig is what I do, not who I am."

"You must be miserable in your professional life."

He laughed. "I enjoy what I do."

"Uh-huh," Ava said eyeing him, as he let out another chuckle. "Did you ever consider maybe I'm just interested in finding out how you spend your days, or what interests you, and not making a snap judgment about your character traits or desirability?"

She met his gaze, challenging him.

"I'm a photographer," he answered in surrender. "Macon doesn't have enough opportunities for me to make a living, so I had to leave."

"You're saying you would've stayed if you could've found a gig?" Ava asked, wrinkling her nose.

He shrugged, fixing her with another one of his grins that affected her breathing. "I like the quiet."

"It's boring," she said, arching a brow.

"It's peaceful."

"It's stale."

"It's real. People in small towns are who they are. I find that to be refreshing."

"I find that to be lame."

He laughed, his eyes raking over her frame again.

"Small towns aren't any better than big cities," Ava said. "You just see people's flaws up close and personal so it feels more authentic, even though it's basically the same crap, just a smaller toilet."

Elias laughed again, his eyes dancing again with appreciation as Ava sipped from her drink.

He bit his lip, still grinning as he eyed her. "I had a crush on you in high school."

"Congratulations?"

He laughed boisterously as she finished off her drink, hiding her smile.

"Come dance with me, Ava."

His voice had dropped an octave and he was staring at her again with eyes that held secrets and depth beneath the playfulness. Boyz II Men's "Let it Snow" had just started playing in the background, and a few more couples were now slow dancing in the living room. Kendrick had dimmed the lights, and the twinkle of the white Christmas lights that hung over the wide fireplace was casting a soft glow in the room now.

"Dance with you?"

"You know how to do that, right? Weren't you a cheerleader?"

"You had a crush on me in high school, remember? You know I was a cheerleader."

He chuckled again, his eyes growing heavy as he openly assessed her.

"Pretty sure I still do... have a crush on you," he clarified when she stared at him.

Unexpectedly, she felt her face flush at his compliment.

"We're both too old for crushes. And you know nothing about me."

"I know enough. And I like what I do know. A lot."

Heat crept into her cheeks again. She rolled her eyes, annoyed with herself. She wasn't a blushing kind of chick. But this dude was not at all shy, and his confidence was arousing. Plus, he was smart and funny and seemed refreshingly genuine. He stood, extending his hand toward her. She put on a show of setting her empty glass on the coffee table in front of her and releasing an audible breath. She touched his hand, charged energy sweeping through her bloodstream at the contact, and let him pull her up.

He moved them to the center of the room, where he pulled her close. Her skin hummed beneath his easy touch, as he glided his hand to the small of her back. His touch wasn't overtly sexual but the implication, the possessiveness, was there. Once again, she questioned her mental state because she was legit turned on. He smelled of *man*— virile, and her body was reacting.

"Ava," he murmured in her ear as he swayed them around the steadily filling makeshift dance floor in the living room. "Come hang out with me tomorrow."

"We met 2.5 seconds ago. You're moving pretty fast don't you think?" Her voice huskier than she intended for it to be but his arms were around her, his strong chest pressed against her softer frame, and she really just wanted to lean into him.

"I don't think I'm moving fast at all. You like me."

She attempted to pull back so she could tell him exactly what she thought of his cocky statement but he pulled her back against him. She felt, rather than saw, his smile.

"And I really, *really* like you," he continued easily, his

voice deep and seductive, causing her breath to hitch. "I'm not interested in wasting time pretendin' like I don't want to immediately spend more time with you."

"Tomorrow is Christmas," she pointed out, her eyes fluttering closed when his nose brushed against the shell of her ear.

"Yeah, and you'd be the best Christmas gift ever."

She grinned, inhaling as he pulled their bodies a little closer.

"Laying it on pretty thick there, guy."

He chuckled and his fingers brushing against the small of her back, against her red sweater dress. "Is it working?"

"No."

He smiled. "Look, how about this-- you hang with your family, I'll hang with mine, and we can go to the late show tomorrow night. I'll even save you a plate. I'm cooking."

She blew out a breath, biting on her lower lip. "You're cooking?" Her tone was disbelieving.

"It's the men's turn this year. Me and my pops and my brothers are on kitchen duty. I'm making the gumbo."

He was tracing his thumb lightly on the small of her back, as he moved them to the music. "Come be my Christmas gift, Ava."

This time she couldn't contain her smile. His ass was charming. That was for sure. "My mom... it's just me and her," she said. "I don't want to leave her alone tomorrow."

Elias shrugged easily, still swaying them to the music. "So, bring her over for dinner."

Ava shook her head. "That's... doing way too much."

"Then we can hang after dinner."

Ava blinked, pushing out a breath.

"Elias."

"Ava."

He smiled down at her, his eyes heavy with desire and intrigue.

"Spend some time with me," he asked again, his breath warm against the shell of her ear. He pulled her completely against him this time and she couldn't deny that she was turned on even if she wanted to. She inexplicably *wanted* to spend more time with him. He seemed to sense her acceptance before she even uttered the words because he smiled.

"I'll pick you up at 7:30 after we both have dinner," he said. "Sound good?"

She shook her head, thoroughly confounded by the turn of events. "Alright."

Elias let out a long breath then, as if he'd been holding it, and Ava smile and relaxed further into his arms. Maybe this party wasn't so boring after all.

TWO

"What?"

"Don't 'what' me... you *know* what."

Ava rolled her eyes at her friend, barely containing her smile as she looked at the passing scenery. Every other house in the small neighborhood was decorated with Christmas lights, though some were struggling to express their love for the holiday more than others. Some houses only had their mailboxes strung with dull white lights; others their front window in an effort to keep up with their neighbors.

"I can't believe you were all cuffed up in the corner with Elias Young."

Ava looked over at Ellie but said nothing as Ellie laughed. Ava hadn't felt "cuffed" at all. She'd felt intrigued. Warm. *Turned-on.* Which is why it was imperative that she cut it off. Immediately.

"I bet you his gumbo will be delicious." Even the way Ellie said "gumbo" sounded sexual, and Ava rolled her eyes. "He's fine, he's professional, and he can probably cook too?"

"Ty was all of those things."

Ellie stared at her and then rolled her eyes.

"Ty was fine but he was movie-star fine. Elias is down-to-earth rescue-you-from-a-burning-house kind of fine."

Ava couldn't hold in her laugh. Elias *was* that rugged kind of good looking with a smile that made him seem as though he could still ramble off Newtown's Law or something.

"The real question is, what's up with you and Kendrick?" Ava deflected. "It took you all of ten minutes to stick your tongue down his throat."

"Correction. He stuck his tongue down *my* throat. And it was delicious."

"Oh, gross!" Ava frowned and laughed, rolling her eyes at her friend.

"Shit, I *needed* that attention," Ellie admitted, running her fingers through her wavy, shoulder-length ringlets, her eyes still on the dark road. "It's lonely out here in these streets."

"Ellie, calm down. You broke up with Rashad like five minutes ago."

"I broke up with Rashad like three weeks ago," Ellie said, flashing her a look. "I can admit that I'm needy."

"Rebound," Ava sang under her breath. She unwrapped one of the many candy canes she'd taken the liberty to remove from the candy dish and popped the tail end into her mouth.

Ellie shrugged. "So? Rebounds are underrated. I see absolutely nothing wrong with indulging in a fine, muscular, did I say *fine* rebound." Ellie looked at her pointedly. "You should too."

Ava rolled her eyes, deflecting again. "But does Kendrick know that he's just a rebound?" Ava asked, glancing at her friend as she made the corner onto the street that Ava had called home throughout most of her childhood.

Ellie shot her a look. "Like he cares."

Ava didn't dispute her friend's assessment. Of course, he didn't care. He was a dude. But Ellie did. She talked tough but was quick to catch feelings. That's how Rashad had lasted so long in spite of his super wack, deadbeat shenanigans. Ava didn't need to share that info with her friend though, because she was well aware. One of the defining points of their friendship, which had been going strong since the ninth grade, was that they were honest with each other. That, and they analyzed themselves to death.

Ava knew her issues, which sometimes trickled over to her relationships. Ellie knew hers as well, pinpointing her sometimes strained relationship with her mom and white stepdad. Ellie's dad was black and her mom was white, and had remarried a white man. It wasn't a big deal except that Ellie always said he was *white*.

"My mom is white but this guy, Sam? He's *white*."

Ellie was convinced he had long harbored issues with her because she identified as black, even though her deep blue-green eyes and thin, curly hair immediately indicated that she was bi-racial. Ellie split her time between her mom's white household, with Sam's two younger daughters, and her dad's, who'd also remarried and had a young son with his new, black wife. Ellie was stretched between two worlds, she often said, though she felt most comfortable at her dad's.

"Tell mama I'll see her tomorrow," Ellie said as she pulled up outside of Ava's mother's modest but cute bungalow. She was planning to come by after she had dinner with her mom. "You're seriously gonna go over there tonight?" Ava asked, quirking an eyebrow at her friend.

"Did you not just hear me tell you that I'm needy? Besides, Kendrick is cool. And he's in real estate. He can probably hook me up."

"Alright," Ava said warningly, pushing the door open. The cool air immediately circled her and she shivered. "See you tomorrow. Love you."

"Love you too," Ellie said, kissing her hand and waving it in Ava's general direction. She waited until Ava made up the short sidewalk to the house and stuck her key in the lock before peeling off way too quickly because it was just beginning to snow.

Ava walked into the house, greeted by warmth and the smell of vanilla. Her mom, Caren, wasn't much in the way of a regular cook but she could bake.

The house had remained virtually the same since she'd left for college, cute and modern, despite its old school exterior. Her mom loved color, and the couch was peach with bright yellow, orange and deep purple pillows decorating it. The art on the walls were mostly from West African artists, with one special piece she'd picked up when she and Ava had taken a trip to Ghana three years ago.

There were a couple of glasses of wine sitting on the coffee table and Ava knew her mom's boyfriend of eight months, Jeff, was over. She'd met him for the first time earlier in the evening and immediately understood exactly how and why her mom was so smitten.

Meeting Jeff in person felt like meeting an old friend. Sure, they'd spoken on the phone a few times prior, and she'd even chatted briefly with him on video during one of her very frequent video chats with her mom, but in person, he was even more charming. And it wasn't practiced charm —it was charm born from confidence, both in himself and his place in life. Jeff was comfortable in his own skin and that radiated from him. He wasn't trying to prove anything; he was good with his station in life and his demeanor announced you could either get on board with that, or not. That by itself was attractive.

He actually reminded her of Elias that way. Ava closed her eyes at the intrusive thought and at the way her belly flipped a little just *thinking* about him. Which is why when that third dance ended, she was happy to get away from him. He smelled way too good; his arms were way too strong, his smile way too relaxed for her to keep up her pretenses much longer.

But it was his conversation, his low baritone in her ear as he talked with her about his job, his life, her life, that had her interested. It was his perspective. It was the fact that even though he was obviously super confident, he also listened and wasn't all about himself. She'd teased Ellie but if she'd danced with him for another song, there was a good chance Elias would've had *her* in some darkened corner, and she would've been a joyful participant.

She bit her lip, as she made her way through the warm living room. It'd only taken a couple of hours with Elias for Ava to feel as though she was already on the verge of getting caught up. And Lord knows she'd already done enough of that with Ty to last a lifetime.

"Hey, Mom," Ava called out as she rounded the corner to the spacious kitchen. "You said you already handpicked the decent Lifetime movies for tonight, right?"

She paused when she entered the kitchen, taking in Caren's worried eyes. Jeff was holding his phone, his expression no more relaxed than her mom's.

"What's going on?" Ava asked frowning, looking at the two of them. Jeff was cool and all but he could definitely catch hands if he'd hurt her mom. Well, maybe not catch *her* hands, seeing as how she was 5'5 on a good day, but he could catch a bat. Or some hot grits.

"Jeff's daughter, Trina, was just in a pretty bad car accident."

Immediately, Ava's stomach dropped. She didn't know Trina of course, but she knew Jeff was close with his daughter and two grandkids, who lived in Savannah. She was actually surprised to still see him at the house since he was planning on driving there to spend Christmas Day with her and her young her daughter.

"Is she okay?"

"She's... stable."

Ava stepped further into the room, placing a hand on her mom's shoulder as she looked at Jeff, who ran a hand over his graying head.

"She has broken ribs, and they had to do surgery on her leg. Reagan and Jackson are fine," her mom said, answering Ava's concerned look. "They weren't in the car. But Jeff is going to have to go now, of course, and look after them for a while."

Ava nodded in understanding, her gaze darting between the two of them, before it hit her.

"It's fine Mom, if you need to go with him," Ava offered. She did mean it. Obviously Jeff's family needed the help. And it was equally obvious from what he wasn't saying that Jeff wanted Caren with him.

"I know we planned to..."

"It's okay Mom, really. I'm a big girl. This is important, clearly."

"You're welcome to come with us," Caren offered, as Jeff nodded.

Sorry as she was for Jeff's daughter, Ava did not want to

spend the holiday crammed in a hospital or babysitting two kids she didn't know.

"Seriously, no worries. I'm good. I promise. Go take care of Trina and her family."

Caren glanced at Jeff, who'd stuffed his hands in his pockets. Although he wanted Caren with him, it was also clear that he wouldn't intrude on the decision-making. Ava's respect for him swelled.

"Well, then what will you do tomorrow?" Caren asked, her small features wrinkled in concern.

Ava stuffed her hands in the oversized pockets of her sweater dress.

"This guy I met, Elias Young, wanted me to hang out with him tomorrow."

At that, her mom raised her brows and grinned.

"Really now."

Ava rolled her eyes. "Yes."

Caren's eyes were lit with interest as she stared at her only daughter.

"And did you agree?"

Ava shifted her weight and looked away, unable to hide her grin.

"Wow. That must've been some party," Caren said, smiling.

"Ellie hooked up with his cousin Kendrick," Ava told her, causing her mom to shake her head and roll her eyes.

"I'm not surprised." She paused, her expression turning serious once more. "So, are you really going to go out tomorrow? It would get you out of the house."

"I'll think about it. Probably," Ava lied.

"You're lying. I think it could be for you to—"

"Good-bye, Mom," Ava interrupted before her mom

could once again warn her to live her life to the fullest and not hold on to "toxic anger" over her failed relationship.

"You guys better get on the road," Ava suggested. "It was already starting to snow a little bit when Ellie dropped me off."

Caren smiled and stepped forward, hugging Ava tightly.

"I love you, daughter."

"I love you more mother."

"And I'll text you so you can tell me about this dude," Caren said discreetly, causing Ava to chuckle.

"You guys be safe, and I'll keep your family in prayer, Jeff."

"I appreciate it, Ava," Jeff said, offering her a brief hug and kiss on the cheek after her mother released her. "Thank you for being so understanding too."

Not thirty minutes later, Ava sank into the deep couch cushions in her mom's living room and flicked on the television. Her life had been in transition for the past three months, ever since she ended things with Ty. Or rather, he ended things by doing what he did. After five years together, five years of her *dealing*, things had ended so dramatically horrible, it was almost surreal. As if she was looking down into her life from above or something because there was no way it could actually be hers.

She'd been adjusting for the past twelve weeks—trying to get some semblance of her life back. Trying to remember who the hell she was, prior to Ty taking up every inch of her life. She moved out of the place they'd been sharing for the past couple of years, into her own little bungalow, which she was renting on the west side of town. And she enjoyed it, getting back to herself. Getting to know herself again without some man up in her grill, burdening her with his wants and expectations.

It only made sense that she was closing out the year doing something she'd never done before in all her thirty-one years—spending the Christmas holiday without her mom. She'd be spending Christmas alone too because she'd definitely made her mind up—she was *not* going anywhere with Elias'. Now that she was away from his presence and his cocky smile, her mind was clearer. And her mind was telling her one thing: *nope*.

She'd turned off the lights in the house, leaving on only the white lights from the Christmas tree and fireplace after changing into her annual Christmas pajamas Caren always bought them—which were soft, comfy and way too big. She took a sip of eggnog, which she'd mixed with a bit of rum as she began watching the cheesy holiday romance her mom had selected. But half the enjoyment of even watching these kinds of flicks was making fun of the utter cheesiness, and with her mom gone, she had no one to crack jokes with. She frowned after five minutes and flicked the channel, stopping only when she came up on her all-time favorite, A *Charlie Brown Christmas*. She smiled as Linus and poor Charlie Brown went off on their venture to pick that pitiful tree that everyone laughed at.

Her phone buzzed and she picked it up, half expecting it to be her mom.

"Ava." She could almost hear Elias' voice saying her name, and she smiled, but only for a second before frowning. She debated if she should respond. But it was probably best since she needed to tell him their date was a no-go anyway.

"Elias."

"You're home safe?" The text came immediately and Ava grinned.

"You're a little late to be asking about my well-being. I could've been in a ditch somewhere by now."

"Are you?"

"Am I what?"

"In a ditch somewhere?"

"If I were in a ditch, I wouldn't have the time to be texting you would I?"

"I don't know what people do in ditches."

Ava laughed aloud.

"You are so not funny."

"But you're laughing right now anyway."

"Nope. I'm actually about to stop texting you because my phone is nearly dead."

"Karma from all that rude reading you were doing at the party."

Ava rolled her eyes, grinning.

"Good night, Elias."

"Sleep well, Ava. See you soon."

Ava sighed, letting her head rest against the back of the couch, her gaze on the Christmas wreath hanging over her mom's small mantel. Her mom could've been a decorator instead of an English professor at the local community college. Ava stared at the lights, thinking of the ones she'd just danced under earlier tonight with Elias. She should call him now and tell him she wasn't going on a date with him ever. That'd be the polite thing to do.

"I'm such a punk," she breathed aloud, just as the lights suddenly clicked off.

She blinked as if that would eliminate the pitch black of the living room.

"You've got to be kidding me."

She reached blindly for her nearly dead phone on the plush couch cushions then shined it over the darkened living room, though it didn't do much in the way of light, and got up from the couch, careful not to bump into the coffee table, as she made her way to the large window by the TV. She sighed loudly and shook her head. The entire block was encased in darkness, which meant the power outage hadn't affected just her. The snow was still coming down in thick sheets, and she peered out the window again, contemplating her options before checking the weather on her phone.

"An ice storm?" she said aloud again, pressing her head against the cold window pane.

The heavy snow had officially been upgraded just twenty minutes ago. Which meant that she was stuck in the house with no power, no heat, and no realistic time frame for any of that to be rectified since it was Christmas Eve. Weighing her options as she went to search for a candle in the kitchen, she quickly dialed Ellie. The phone went straight to voicemail, probably because she'd turned it off to get her freak on with Kendrick. She tried her one more time, but again was met with Ellie's bubbly voice telling her to leave a message.

"Fan-freaking-tastic," she muttered. She checked the weather in Atlanta. It was cold but the skies were clear.

The temperature was already beginning to dip in the house, just that fast, and she stuffed her hands in her pajama pockets, trying to think. Ellie wasn't answering the phone and she literally knew no one else in the town. Her mom had friends that she could probably technically call if she knew their numbers, which she didn't. And staying in the freezing cold house wasn't happening either. Yeah, she was going home. Tonight. If she left now, she could beat the storm before it hit since it was moving into the town from the opposite direction of Atlanta. Once she got on the freeway, just a few miles outside of the city, she'd be good.

Armed with a new plan, even if it was admittedly kind of a crap one, Ava quickly made her way up the stairs and packed her clothes. She'd only been there for a day, so the packing took all of five minutes since it was dark and she was trying to move quickly. She did a quick walk-through and blew out the candle she'd lit and left on the kitchen counter, but not before she stuffed the sugar cookies from the reindeer plate on the stovetop into a baggie and crammed them into her purse. No use in Christmas being completely ruined.

A minute later, Ava slid out of the front door into the frigid cold. She'd call her mom once she was on the highway, because she didn't want to worry her when she already had so much on her plate.

She slid into her car and immediately turned the ignition, blasting the heat, even though it was currently coming out cold. *Damn, this Christmas sucks.* The only highlight so far had been Elias, and there was a good chance she'd never even see him again. Once he realized she'd not only blew him off but had driven back to Atlanta without a peep, Ava was pretty sure whatever interest he'd previously expressed would be done for. Not that she cared.

The streets were a whisper when she turned out of the dark neighborhood. After just seeing it all lit up for Christmas it was weird seeing the houses pitch black. She could barely even make out their outlines. She quickly flicked on her high beams, which helped some but not really. Literally, no one was on the streets— the business lights were off, and for a second, she was scared. She paused at the street light for no reason, since it was down too, took a deep breath, and kept going. She was out of options and she was grown ass woman, not a character in some Christmas ghost movie. She actually saw a flick like that last year, when her mom had come to visit. It was the stupidest thing ever.

Finally, she came to the exit that led to the interstate, turning her wipers on triple time because it was snowing so hard. Two hours ago, there was no way you could've told her she'd be driving her car, which needed to have the tires rotated, back to Atlanta at nine o'clock at night on Christmas Eve. She blew out a breath, squinting out of the windshield because she could barely see the asphalt through all the snow. There seemed to be only one other car on the highway, though it was a good fifty feet in front of her and she could barely make out the taillights.

She chewed her lip, trying to calm herself down because driving in these conditions was scary, and she was only doing thirty miles per hour. The yellow line dividing the highway lanes was completely invisible. Unexpectedly, she hit a small bump and immediately, she felt as though she was starting to slide. Her heart began thumping in her chest. She hit the brakes and suddenly, she was spinning.

"Oh my God!" she yelped, gripping the steering wheel tighter, as she frantically pumped the brakes, trying desperately to control the wheel. But that only made it worse. She'd completely lost control and the car continued to spin... she closed her eyes and screamed.

THREE

Ava opened one eye-lid, testing to see if she was still alive. The car was dark and she couldn't see much, so she opened the other eyelid too, breathing a sigh of relief. She hadn't even hit anything- she'd just finally stopped spinning, thank the Lord. She looked around, her heart still thudding in her chest, though it did feel as though her adrenaline was starting to slow. She groaned aloud and banged her head against the steering wheel. She was in a ditch. Inhaling, she lifted her head, peering around her and hit the gas. The wheels screeched and the engine revved as if it really did want to move but nothing happened.

"*Crap! Crap! Crap!*"

She beat her fist against the steering wheel before taking a deep breath. Beating the steering wheel wasn't going to do anything except hurt her hand. Besides, it wasn't the steering wheel's fault that she'd stupidly tried to drive in the middle of a full-on ice storm. Maybe she *was* like one of those dense characters in the stupid Christmas movies she used to laugh at after all.

Quickly, she pushed open the door and stepped out into the freezing cold. It was the kind of cold that immediately made your face ache. The kind of cold that made your eyes tear. She imagined herself instantly freezing over like in that goofy end of the world movie with Jake Gyllenhaall, *The Day After Tomorrow*.

She pulled the hood up on her too thin, leather jacket that really was mostly for just looking cute, not staying warm, and walked around the car to inspect the damage. Her car was slightly tilted in the ditch, but she hadn't hit anything, so there were no dents. But her car was definitely stuck and would need a tow truck to get out. Stuffing her hands into her pockets, since she wasn't wearing gloves, she attempted to climb out of the ditch, slipping and sliding in the snowy mud and grassy weeds before she was able to make it out.

The snow was blinding, coming down hard, sideways, not in soft little pillow waves like on TV, darting her cheeks with tiny ice pellets. This snow was on a damn mission. She sniffed, looking back at her car to make sure the door hadn't shut on her, and then peered into the darkened highway, careful to stand as far away from the asphalt as possible in case a random car or truck drove by, since she was sure no one would be able to see her dumb ass. She stood there for a second, then finally shook her head, and hurried back down the hill to her car, hopping back inside and shivering as she held her hands in front of the heater.

She pulled out her phone, trying to think rationally. At least the heat was on but she'd left with only one-third tank of gas, figuring that she could fill up at the cheaper gas station, just a few miles outside of town. With no heat, there was definitely a chance that she'd end up freezing to death.

Within in the next hour, probably. In an ice storm. On Christmas Eve.

"Crap!" she exclaimed again.

She looked at her phone, her eyes widening.

"You've got to be kidding me."

The phone life was at three percent. She wiggled the wire to her car charger, then jerked it again. She pulled it from her phone blew on it like a Nintendo cartridge then put it in again. Nothing. Her heart, once again, kicked into overdrive. No phone meant no way to contact anyone. And she was at least fifteen miles outside of town. The snow was still falling relentlessly, as if it was on personal a mission to cover the entire town in as little time as possible. There was no way she could walk anywhere in these conditions.

She sighed and called Ellie again.

"Please pick up..." she muttered to herself, selfishly praying that Kendrick had said or done something stupid so that Ellie would've gotten mad enough to turn on her phone on like a sane person. She cursed when Ellie's bubbly voicemail came on again.

"Ugh, you suck Ellie," she groaned.

She stared at the battery on her phone. Two percent. *Dammit. Dammit.* Okay, what was the most logical thing to do here, Lord? She could call AAA. But she wasn't even a member any more— it'd expired last July, and by the time she used her phone to search for the number, talk to a customer service representative to order the service, and then tell them where she was, her phone would definitely be dead.

She glanced out of the darkened window, rubbing the glass to see out of it better, though she didn't know why. She couldn't see jack shit.

"Just do it, Ava, and stop being stupid."

She bit her lip and called the only other person she could think to call. He answered on the second ring, his timber warm and comforting when he said her name.

"So, um, remember that ditch we were talking about earlier? Well, I'm in it."

FOUR

What in the hell was she thinking?

Elias asked himself the question for the fourth time in the past sixty seconds, as he carefully maneuvered his dad's F-150 through the snow-filled streets toward the interstate exit.

This wasn't cute snow, the kind that he'd maybe want to shoot later. Nah, this snow was destructive, falling almost angrily, like the apocalypse had hit. This kind of snowfall was a rarity in Georgia. It only happened once every seven years or so though lately, with global warming, it seemed more like every two years. His younger brother, Matthew, would argue it was the government's weather machines that had it snowing like Wisconsin in the south. Matthew was all about a good conspiracy theory, though these slick streets had Elias leaning toward his line of thinking tonight. He squinted out the window onto the wet asphalt, turning his wipers up another notch.

He couldn't believe Ava actually got her ass in the car and tried to drive in this craziness. It was bad out here and freezing. And she was alone in the dark, on the side of the road in a ditch, with no phone because it went dead right as she was telling him where she was. He almost smiled as he thought about the first thing she said when she called him— she managed to keep her sense of humor, even in dire circumstances, he had to give her that.

He'd been caught off guard by Ava's presence at Kendrick's party. He literally hadn't seen her since high school, in person anyway. Social media made it impossible to be completely obscure, so she'd popped up on his timeline every now then, and when she appeared, he always caught himself smiling.

Every dude in school knew who Ava Ramseur was. She was the girl everybody wanted—from the video game geeks, to the ball players, to the wanna be gangsters and the dudes like him, who didn't really fall into any category at all, but wandered around trying on new activities and interests like socks.

Ava was gorgeous, even back then. The kind of pretty that wouldn't dull when she got deep into her 20s, like a lot of women who were cute as teenagers, but were only average as adults. And even from afar, she'd seemed... superior. Not conceited but more like she was too sophisticated for high school. That was it. At seventeen, he'd pegged her as pretty but kinda stuck up.

When he saw her again tonight though, he briefly struggled to remember why he never tried to holler at her back then. Being stuck up wasn't a real deterrent for his horny-ass teenage self. So why hadn't he ever tried to catch Ava's attention?

"You remember what you were like in high school, bro," Kendrick laughed when Elias asked the question aloud. *"She wasn't on your radar like that."*

Elias laughed too because it was true. At sixteen and

seventeen he was into the "fast" girls—the type of chicks his mom always warned him "better not come up pregnant." The girls who let him get it in the darkened parking lot behind the rec center on MLK and who stole shit out of the Polo section of Dillard for him.

But that was then. A lifetime ago. Holding Ava close earlier tonight while they danced felt almost like high school—familiar in a way that had him talking more than usual, teasing her, just to see how long she was gonna play like she wasn't feeling him a little bit.

Elias grinned to himself as he made his way onto the interstate, as faded images of Ava back then flooded his mind, mixing with the new ones he'd imprinted on his brain tonight after spending less than an hour in her company.

He was only intending to flirt with her a little bit, kill a little time—get his mind off things he didn't want to linger on this holiday.

Last year, Christmas time had been rough. He tried to keep it moving, tried not to let himself be weighed down by memories and "what ifs" but his pain came through anyway. He was irritable and moody. Snappy with his staff. And when he came home last year, spent most of the time drunk. Nothing sloppy but definitely inebriated. Seeing Ava tonight—someone who had nothing to do with those memories, was refreshing.

He figured she'd be game to entertain him, at least a little, since she was so obviously disinterested in what was going on around her. Her entire demeanor had emitted nothing but pure boredom from the time she arrived at Kendrick's. She kept looking at her girl, who Kendrick had cuffed up in the corner and picking at her wavy hair as she people watched, brushing off dudes with polite but disinterested smiles.

Elias had checked her out for a full half hour while he half-listened to his boy, JJ, tell him about his latest life dilemma with his baby mama, Melissa, a chick he'd gotten pregnant a few years after they graduated, and hadn't quite mustered up the will to marry or completely let go. JJ was going on and on about Melissa's new dude "being around his kid" as if he hadn't had almost ten years to lock her down and avoid his current situation. JJ was cool but he was made of nothing but Newports and self-manufactured drama, and Elias was pretty much content to only vibe with dude once a year these days. Back in the day, in high school, they'd kicked it pretty heavy, both of them disappointing their parents with teenage boy shenanigans—selling weed, skipping school to play video games or sneak girls into JJ's crib. It was only the grace of God that kept them out of juvie. That and JJ's pops was a local cop, of all things.

But once Elias got his head on straight, he knew that making a life in Macon wasn't in the cards. It wasn't just that he couldn't find work— it was also that he knew if he stayed, he'd be stuck in rut. Trapped kicking it with the same dudes, who did the same things, making the same poor life choices because it was the only thing there was to do and no one seemed to want to know any better. He honestly did like the quiet life of a small town but... nah. He had to break out, and he felt it every time he came home and did things like hit up his cousin's annual party, which is partly why he'd immediately noticed Ava when she arrived. After about twenty minutes of people watching and sipping her drink, she'd thrown him completely. She pulled out her phone and started *reading*. He had to go talk to her after that.

And once he' found out that she was reading *The Road*? That wasn't ordinary casual reading. While they danced they got to talking about the book again, and once more, she'd impressed him by making an immediate comparison to Octavia Butler's *Parable* series, which was one of his favorites. She'd wondered how much the author, Cormack McCarthy, was inspired by one of the most prominent black women sci-fi writers, and rather or not he'd acknowledged her influence at all. He realized Ava wasn't stuck up, even a little bit. She was sophisticated but accessible. Like back in high school she maybe would've smoked out with you but chastised you for missing class because of it.

And then, they'd started talking about entertainment and her job as a publicist at a women's-centered cable network. Mostly, she worked reality shows and the occasional soap-opera drama, which he'd been somewhat surprised to learn she was disinterested in.

"I'm only doing this until I can launch my own company and focus on things more relevant to my interests," she'd told him as they swayed to the music.

"And what's relevant to your interests, Ava?"

She smiled when he asked that, and it made him pull her a little closer as they danced.

"Pop culture."

"I thought you were about to say something profound. You had me listening all intently for that?" he'd laughed, teasing her. *"Isn't that what you already do?"*

She'd wrinkled her nose in distaste, and he'd smiled because it was adorable and sexy, and all she'd done was make a face.

"Entertainment is important too, especially in our pop-culture driven society. The things entertainment projects, the subtle way it influences our perspective... It might be one of the absolutely most important aspects of our socialization, in

America at least, because everyone wants to think it's innocent."

"The subtle is sometimes more powerful than the overt," he'd offered, earning him an excited *"Exactly!"* from Ava.

Most women's eyes grew wider when they were trying to impart something they deemed important but not Ava's. Hers narrowed a bit, lowered, as if under the weight of whatever she was about to say.

" I don't want to just promote crappy TV shows anymore. I want to work with people in film and television who I feel are putting out great work that would be overlooked otherwise. People who are humanizing the stories and experiences of black people across the diaspora."

She'd proceeded to tell him about an Atlanta-based director she was working with on the side to get her short film noticed. Her eyes lit up as she described the film about the alarming mortality rates of black women during child birth.

"Black mothers are 12 times more likely to die than white mothers. Black people's pain literally isn't taken seriously by doctors. This film exposes that through this incredible story about a woman living in Atlanta who died two weeks after giving birth.

He'd listened intently. Not just because the film sounded powerful, but because Ava's enthusiasm made him want to hear about everything that excited her.

He couldn't remember feeling so drawn to a woman so quickly beyond sexually, anyway, in ages. Not since Janay. He'd been thinking about Ava non-stop since they parted ways. He even got all stalker with it, hitting up her social media pages when he got back to the house. He was kinda trying to talk himself out of being so intrigued so quickly. Social media usually always did it. People went out of their way to project their best selves but nine times out of ten, ended up doing the exact opposite—exaggerating their flaws because they were trying too hard.

Instead, Elias found himself impressed all over again because as pretty as she was, Ava didn't have a bunch of pictures posted of herself. Instead, she did things like take pictures of objects or things that she found interesting or took pictures of herself out and about on the scene she probably frequented for work but only made herself partially visible. Her pictures were artistic and showcased her creativity, not vanity. He realized, with appreciation, that she had a good eye.

And then she'd called him and said she was in a damn *ditch* on the side of the road at ten at night. He narrowed his eyes, slowing even more as he approached the markers she'd given him. She said she'd made it just past the first mile marker before she started spinning.

Elias spotted what had to be Ava's car just a few seconds later and breathed a sigh a relief as he parked on the side of the road. He turned on his emergency lights and climbed out of his dad's truck, the cold immediately hitting him, harsh and fast. Quickly as he could without slipping on the soggy, mud-drenched weeds, he made his way down the ditch, toward her car—a Toyota Camry that looked fairly new—struggling to see through the snow.

He could barely make out her silhouette when he approached her window. He tapped on it quickly then stuffed his hands in his pockets, ducking his head in an attempt to dodge the combative snow fall. And she... rolled down the window. Like she was at a drive-through and he was here to take her order.

"Thank God it's just you," she answered, heaving a sigh of relief, causing her breath to puff in the air. She had a stocking cap on pulled down low on her head and was wearing nothing but a leather jacket that he knew couldn't have been doing much in the way of keeping her warm.

"Hey," he said, offering her a half-smile because he could see now she looked frightened. "You okay?" Her dark eyes were wide and wary, as if she were looking at an apparition.

"I'm okay now that you're really here," she answered, heaving a sigh of relief. He almost asked if she thought he wouldn't show up but stopped when he saw her breath puff in the air, even though she pulled her head back into the car as she reached into the passenger side seat for her bag. He tilted his head, the rush of the falling snow beating against his back.

"You didn't have the heat on?"

She shivered and shrugged, hoisting the bag onto her shoulder. "I was almost out of gas. I had to ration it."

She at least had the good sense to look ashamed. "Thank you for coming, Elias."

He grinned, though it was painful because it was so cold and his face muscles were practically frozen.

"Come on before you turn into an ice cube."

He quickly opened the door for her, waiting as she rolled up the window once more and grabbed a roller suitcase from the front seat. He took her hand, helping her out of the car, and she fell against his chest. She looked up at him, her breath forming a cloud in the cold.

"Thank you," she said softly, again.

"You're welcome."

He could see his own breath brush against her upturned mouth, her chest pressed against his, rising and falling in rhythm with the snow. She stood on her tiptoes, pressing her lips against his cool cheek.

"Come on," he said grinning, sliding his hand to hers, "before we freeze."

He quickly made his way up the mild incline of the ditch, pulling her gently along with him. It was slippery though, and he pulled her close, pushing her in front of him with a steadying hand on her back so he could catch her if she started to tumble. They made it to his truck, and he hurriedly swung the passenger door open for her, helping her climb inside before he jogged around to the driver's side and slid in, after placing her suitcase in the backseat.

Elias sat in the seat for a second, trying to feel his fingers. He sniffed and glanced over at Ava, his stomach sinking at the thought that she' been sitting in that freezing car for at least an hour. The inside of the cab was dark, save for the lights on his dashboard, but he could plainly see that her nose was red, her cheeks flushed. She was sitting stiffly, feebly waving her hands in front of the heater. He was glad he had the presence of mind to leave the truck running, so it was toasty inside of the cab, though Ava obviously wasn't feeling it yet. He took off his gloves then scooted closer to the passenger seat and reached for her bare hands.

"This'll help them warm up faster," he said when she looked up at him with surprise. She pulled her bottom lip between her teeth but didn't object, as he gathered her small hands between his, rubbing and massaging warmth back into them.

"Damn, Ava. You're *frozen*," he said, working his way over her palms, then massaging each individual finger to bring back circulation. Her fingers were soft, as if she'd never done a day of hard work in her life, never washed a dish.

"Can you feel your fingers yet?"

"Almost." She smiled as he kept working on them.

"Your hands are really soft."

"Thank you." She smiled without looking up at him, though he did see her brows were raised.

"What? You have pretty hands. Like a pianist," he observed as he continued massaging, lingering at the creases between her fingers. She pushed out a small laugh, her eyes still on his fingers as he massaged her hands.

"That's not creepy at all. Is this the part where you tell me you want to cut them off and keep them forever in your freezer?"

A burst of laughter escaped him and she smiled up at him, those hypnotic onyx black eyes of hers playful and, he realized, inviting.

"You have a smart-ass mouth, Ava."

He said it matter-of-factly and she chuckled, her willowy laughter softly bouncing throughout the darkened truck cab.

"I've been told that a time or two," she admitted, still smiling.

Now that he wasn't freezing, he noticed that she'd scrubbed her face free of the make-up she had on at the party. *Pretty as hell.* Her lashes were long and thick, and her eyes were slightly hooded as if she was in possession of some deep secret that she was just a second away from revealing.

"Does it always get you in trouble?" he asked.

"What?"

"Your smart mouth."

She shook her head as she met his eyes, hers teasing.

"Nope. The opposite. My mouth usually gets me *out* of trouble."

He smirked and his gaze skirted to her lips—which for this second at least, were his favorite feature—full and soft, her top lip poking out more than her bottom, gently curved like they were made specifically for kissing. He felt more than heard the small hitch in Ava's breathing when he raised his gaze back to hers, saw the new awareness in her eyes as she realized the implication behind her words.

"Stop, Elias." She rolled her eyes and smiled as he chuckled.

"What?" he grinned and she rolled her eyes again, though she made no attempt to remove her hands from his.

"You good yet?" his voice was low, and Ava touched her tongue to the corner of her mouth, wiggling her fingers then nodded.

Reluctantly, he released her hands, repositioning himself behind the steering wheel. It was already going to take them an hour or more for a fifteen-mile ride and they needed to get a move on.

"I can't believe this weather," Ava said, shaking her head as she peered out of the passenger window, rubbing her hands over arms again, pressing toward the vents once more.

"There's hot chocolate in that thermos for you." He nodded his head toward the cup holder as he pulled onto the highway. "It'll warm you up some."

"You brought me hot chocolate?"

Her surprise was evident and he grinned.

"Wow, thank you."

"You're welcome."

She lifted the thermos and took a long sip, humming her pleasure.

"This is *so* good," she said, her surprise evident once more.

Hell, he'd bring her hot chocolate every day of the week just to hear that sound of satisfaction from her, or to see her eyes gloss over with pure bliss, the way they were now.

She was quiet for a while as he maneuvered down the slippery interstate, and he didn't know if it was because she was still frozen or if she was still shaken up from being stranded. He knew why he wasn't talkative—it was slick as hell outside, and he was driving on black ice as he crept along the deserted highway, praying they wouldn't end up stuck out here. It was that bad.

"Hey, Elias?"

Ava's honeyed voice floated through the quiet cab and he broke his concentration momentarily to glance over at her.

"Thank you," she said again, inhaling as she met his gaze, her eyes serious. "I mean it. I don't know what would've happened if you hadn't answered. So, thank you."

He smiled. "It's no problem, Ava. You call, I'll come."

FIVE

Damn, damn, damn, he was *fine*.

She'd thought Elias was good-looking at the party—fit, bedroom eyes, pretty lips. But nope. She'd been mistaken. Because now, behind the wheel of a truck in his hoodie and black pea coat, he was gorgeous. Action movie star gorgeous. Athlete endorsement deal gorgeous. Throw you up against the wall and make love to you with your panties pulled to the side gorgeous.

Ava reluctantly turned and looked out of the window, mentally shooing away her treacherous thoughts. Scenarios she had no business imagining. But unable to help herself, she looked at Elias out of the corner of her eye again. His facial hair made his lips even more noticeable; they were full and well-shaped, matching those sleepy-sexy eyes of his perfectly. He even had a small dimple in his right cheek that showed up only when he was smiling genuinely.

She'd barely gotten a glimpse of him when he knocked on her window, while she sat freezing in her car like a dummy. But when he took her hand, firmly pulling her up the hill and then grabbed her hands once they were inside of the truck— *Lord.* Then he'd started massaging her fingers and even though they were cold, she felt it. She'd felt Elias' touch to the very tip of her toes, just as she had when she'd briefly kissed his rough cheek. So much so, she had to crack a joke to get herself together, which in retrospect didn't help much because the deep timbre of his laugh was just as arousing as his spontaneous hand massage.

She chewed on the inside of her lip, watching the passing scenery. They were creeping along at a snail's pace but Ava trusted Elias was doing what was necessary to keep them safe since the snow hadn't let up at all.

"The Christmas Song" came on, somehow making the confines of the cab feel smaller, warmer.

"This is my favorite Christmas song of all time," she told him dreamily, eyes still on the road.

"Nope. 'This Christmas' Donny Hathaway," he countered, tossing a half-grin her way.

"Nat King Cole is classic," she told him, arching a brow.

"So is Donny."

"Yeah but Nat King Cole is *classic* classic."

He grinned that cocky but alluring smile again. "So is Donny."

"Yeah, but he's *new* classic."

"What does that even mean, Ava?" he asked, arching a thick brow. The way he said her name, the familiarity in which said it, had her shifting on the seat again.

"It means I'm right," she managed. "And you're not."

He chuckled and she finally pulled her hat off her head. Elias looked over at her. It was one of those kinds of looks that said he liked what he saw, very much. She shifted in her seat and his smile increased knowingly before he returned his attention to the road. He was cocky but it was warranted. There was a connection between them, undoubtedly. A connection and familiarity that was buzzing and humming now that they were in the intimate confines of the warm truck. The same way it had while they'd slow danced at that dry party.

Elias' phone buzzed between them and he grabbed it off the seat, answering it without taking his eyes off the road.

"What's up. Yep." He glanced over at her and smiled. "She's straight."

She smiled because he was and he chuckled a little, wondering who he was talking to.

"Alright. About another hour or so."

Ava's eyes widened. They were only a few miles outside of Macon and it was going to take a full hour?

"Yeah, I will. Peace," Elias said, wrapping up the quick conversation.

"My brother, Jeremiah," he informed her as he tossed the phone back onto the seat beside him. "Wanted to make sure I got to you before you turned into a snow cone."

Ava smiled. "Thank you again, Elias, for leaving your family and—"

"It's cool," he interrupted her, glancing over at her, the shadows from the darkened highway dancing over his handsome features. "I was trying to think up a way to see you again tonight anyway. So, that ditch was a win for me."

Ava laughed and shook her head, her belly warming.

"But for real. What's up with you venturing out in Snowpocalypse?" he finally asked, his warm baritone breaking over the soft sounds of the music.

She hesitated.

"You were gonna disappear on me, huh? Leave me hangin' for our date?"

"No."

"No?" He cocked a brow at her.

"I mean, I wasn't going to leave you hanging... I was..."

She stopped abruptly when the truck jerked, lurching to the left on the slick asphalt. Elias was immediately on high alert, cursing softly under his breath, rolling the wheel gently in the opposite direction as the truck attempted to spin, the loud highway markers indicating they were too close to the edge. Ava didn't even realize her hand was gripping his thigh until she looked down, trying to calm her breathing once they were safely back in the proper lane.

"It's really slick out here," she said unnecessarily, as he placed a hand over hers on his leg, in an obvious attempt to calm her.

"Yeah, we're driving on pure ice right now," he answered, his serious gaze still on the road.

She gasped softly and looked down out of the window.

"Black ice," he explained with a half grin at her expression. "You can't see it."

"That's probably what happened to me.... I skidded and started spinning." She was acutely aware of his hand still over hers, wondering how she could be so turned on by the simple gesture, especially given the circumstances. He fixed a look on her that made her feel chastised and... protected.

"It's a blessing you weren't seriously hurt."

"I know."

"The power went off at my mom's," she finally offered. "She'd left unexpectedly out of town because her boyfriend had a family emergency—his daughter was in a pretty bad wreck. I figured I could probably beat the storm. Clearly, I was mistaken."

He frowned. "You were at your mom's alone with no power, Ava?"

He removed his hand from hers and ran it over his head

frowning. "You know you could've called me then. I would've come and got you."

He glanced at her again, his gaze more serious than she'd seen it in the past few hours, and it turned her on.

"So, you're staying with me tonight, right?"

His baritone was low when he asked the question, and even though he likely hadn't meant to sound so sexy when he asked the question, he certainly did. She shifted in her seat and looked out at the snowy road.

"I'm not dropping you back off at a house with no power," he told her when a few long seconds ticked by and she still hadn't replied.

She'd only thought briefly about what she would do once Elias actually picked her up. Her thoughts had primarily been focused on staying warm and not panicking. But staying at his parent's home? Overnight?

"You're good with me, alright?"

He was in her head again and she glanced over at him.

"My family is chill and the house is storm-proof. My dad is a little bit of a survivalist, so even if the power does go out, we won't be out of commission. You'll be safe there and we have the extra space."

He turned and looked at her, his expression saying there wasn't much room for argument.

"Okay." What else was she going to do? "Thank you."

They were quiet for a while as he concentrated on maintaining control of the truck on the slick road. Beneath the headlights, safe in Elias' truck, the snow no longer looked so intimidating. It was actually beautiful, dream-like as it swirled and fell against the blackened sky, in a rhythm all its own.

"So, what were you doing before I became your damsel in distress?" she asked.

He smiled.

"Finishing the gumbo," he glanced at her. "Thinking about you. I wasn't ready to leave you earlier." She looked at him and grinned.

Their gazes held for too long and it felt as if he was seeing too much, namely that she felt the same.

"You really cooked gumbo?"

He smiled again at her abrupt subject change but played along. "I really did. I told you it's our turn to cook this year."

"And you have three brothers? No sisters?"

"Nope. All boys. Nothing but testosterone."

"Where do you fall in age?"

She sipped her cocoa. From his personality, he was probably somewhere in the middle. He was accommodating but knew how to demand attention.

"The middle kinda," he answered, and she smiled. "The twins—Daniel and Jeremiah— are the oldest, then me, then my little brother Matthew."

"If you tell me your mom and dad's names are Joseph and Mary..."

Elias laughed heartily, warming her insides because his smile was so full of life and completely uninhibited. She turned so that she could see him better, her back leaning slightly against the truck door as she cradled the thermos with both hands.

"Nah," he said, refocusing the road. "My mom's name is Hope and my dad's name is Joe. They're just very..."

"Biblical?"

He laughed again. "Something like that. They just wanted to give us names that stood for something."

Ava nodded. "That's respectable. I just can't believe I don't remember you guys. Four brothers in this town?"

It was practically impossible that she couldn't remember crossing paths with him, or at least one of his brothers.

"Macon's not *that* small."

"Yea but..." she trailed off, keeping herself from saying that if his brothers looked anything like him, there was no way she would've forgot them.

"You really only would've known me, anyway," he said. "The twins were in college by the time we moved here my senior year. And Matthew is four years behind me..."

"And it's not like I really ever came back to visit after I left for school."

"Right," Elias said. "And as you so unpretentiously pointed out, we ran in different circles."

Ava laughed, eyeing him. "Because you were a senior when I was a freshman."

He smirked. "Nah, don't try to clean it up now."

"Shut up," she said, swatting at his leg.

"For real though. It was probably a little more than an age difference," he admitted, casting a smirk her way.

"You said that like you were a trouble maker."

"I was," he admitted with a chuckle. "A little bit. I had a few suspensions. Tried to sell a little weed. Got put in an alternative school for the second semester of senior year."

"You sold drugs?" she said in mock surprise.

He grinned and eyed her. "I sold *weed*. But I wasn't very good at it. I was just trying whatever I could. Trying to see what fit."

"Middle child syndrome," she said airily.

"You analyzin' me, Ava?"

"Just making a friendly observation, Elias."

He grinned again, his eyes roaming over her.

"So, what about you? Any brothers or sisters?"

"I have one brother, through my dad. My parents have been divorced since I was two."

Elias nodded, his eyes still on the road. "Let me guess... You're the youngest?"

His gaze was assessing, grin cocky.

"Why would you guess that?"

Elias grinned, eyeing the road. "Seems like you're used to getting your way."

"Seems like you're used to making incorrect judgments about people's personalities."

He chuckled she arched a brow.

"So, you're the oldest?"

"Sorta kinda." She hated this part of the conversation. You'd think she'd be over it by now, but the feeling lingered in the far back of her mind. Elias glanced at her curiously.

"My brother and I are two weeks apart. So, I'm technically older."

Elias glanced at her but said nothing. To his credit, his facial expression didn't change much as he took in the information that her father had been unfaithful to her mom in the worst possible way.

"My dad ended up marrying my brother's mother after he and my mom finally divorced," Ava volunteered, though she didn't know why. Something about Elias, maybe the intelligence in his eyes, was making her talkative. Or maybe it was being in the confines of this truck, smelling his warm, woodsy scent, the intimate feel of being on a barren highway.

"Are you close with your brother?"

Ava smiled, her eyes still fixed on the falling snow.

"Actually, I am. We grew up in different parts of the country," she said, looking at Elias' profile. "His mom moved them to Kansas to be with her family after my dad got her pregnant, but we always had a really great bond. It makes sense with us being so close in age, I guess. 'Ghetto twins,' as people at school used to call it when they found out."

Elias frowned, casting another look her way. "People are corny."

"People *are* corny," Ava agreed. She used to get embarrassed then angry when she was younger until she learned that people are going to judge, no matter what you have going on. It's how too many people build themselves up, on the judgment of others.

"Is he in public relations too then?" Elias was asking.

"No, he's an athlete. He plays basketball."

"Professionally?"

Ava nodded.

"Really?" Elias said, nodding his head, clearly impressed. That was pretty much the reaction of every guy she ever shared that information with. "What's his name?"

"Kyle Ramseur."

Elias' eyes widened slightly. It was always questionable rather or not people would recognize her brother's name. He'd been in the league for a while now but he was a six man and wasn't necessarily on name recognition status with casual fans of the game.

"Kyle Ramseur, who just signed to the Mavs?"

"Yep," Ava said, expecting to him to launch into a full-on conversation about him, or pretend vague disinterest so *she'd* volunteer information about him.

"Cool. He's having a good season," Elias said.

"He is," she said smiling as she thought of Kyle, who said he was already liking Dallas a lot better than Orlando.

"I'd spend summers out in Kansas with him. They lived in a town called Manhattan. When we got older, I'd talk my dad and stepmom into letting me travel with the team to his tournaments in Kansas City."

She laughed, memories of hot days spent with Kyle on the almost two hour-long bus ride into KC.

"That must've sucked for him," Elias laughed, glancing at her. "I'm sure he stayed into it with his teammates over you."

Ava shook her head. "I was kind of a late bloomer."

He raised a brow, allowing his gaze to roam over her.

"I remember you in high school, Ava."

"Not *physically*," she said rolling her eyes, though her body heated at the way he was looking at her. "I liked guys and all of that but not... I was never boy crazy like a lot of my friends were. My life definitely didn't revolve around trying to get their attention."

"Because you didn't have to work for it," Elias surmised.

She shrugged. "I was just interested in other things. Like, when I hung with Kyle, I was aware that I was traveling with a bunch of guys who girls drooled over but I was honestly more into the game. I used to think I was going to be a sports writer since I was too uncoordinated to play myself."

"But you ended up being a cheerleader—you couldn't have been too uncoordinated."

"I could move okay but I wasn't a ball player, at all. I actually only tried out for cheerleading because my friends and I— Ellie who was at the party—and this girl named Alaska, decided we wanted to blacken up the squad."

Elias laughed, furrowing his brow. "For real?"

"Yep. Ellie always wondered why there were never any black cheerleaders on varsity so we made it a point to try out," she explained. "There at least twelve of us who tried out and five of us made the cut on a cheers quad of nine. We were happy with those numbers."

Elias grinned. "So, you were a little revolutionary."

Ava chuckled and shrugged. "Not really but you know," she lifted her shoulders again, smiling.

"That's what's up, though," he said, glancing at her with appreciation. "Now that I'm thinking about it, the cheerleaders were extra blonde before you."

"They haven't had an all-white squad since," Ava said, unable to keep the pride out of her voice, even if the feat was relatively small.

"What about you and your dad then?" Elias asked after a long second. "Are you two close?"

Ava nodded, sipping from the thermos.

"We are," she answered swallowing. "He has his ways, obviously, but he was always there for me. He tried really hard to stick it out with my mom—tried to make up for his indiscretions. He really tried to make it work for our family. But... the heart wants what it wants. And his wanted Kyle's mom. I can't fault him for that. My mom is over it, and so am I. And as I said, he's always been active in my life. I never felt like I came second or anything."

"You're his only girl," Elias said as if that explained everything. "My mom would've killed for a baby girl. I think she slick tried to turn my baby brother Matthew into one."

She laughed. He grinned, eyes on the road. "Had the little dude enrolled in ballet and everything. My dad came home and had a *fit*. Said no son of his was gonna be doing pliés."

Ava laughed again, waving her fingers in front the heating vent, not for the warmth, but for something to do with her hands.

"She didn't try the whole athletes need to know how to

balance argument? Like how football players practice ballet?"

"She tried but Matthew's never been into sports. He wasn't even playing ball or anything close to it at the time, so it was like, dude was *only* in ballet. Dad was like, *nope*, and it was a wrap after that."

Ava laughed again, and Elias chuckled along with her, warming her insides.

"Would you let your son do ballet?" He smirked and she arched a brow.

"I mean, I wouldn't put him *in* the shit. But if he came home and said that's what he wanted to do," Elias shrugged. "I'm not about hindering anyone's progress."

"Uh-huh."

"I'm for real," he insisted, smiling that half-grin that made her palms a little sweaty. "Following your path is important."

Ava smiled, biting the inside of her lip.

"So, what about you? Do you want a house full of boys too whenever you have kids?" she asked.

If she wasn't staring at him so hard, she would've missed the subtle change in Elias' expression, the tightening of his mouth, the way his jaw slightly twitched.

Ava sat up in her seat slightly, staring at him. *If this man had kids and was ashamed to claim them....*

"Do you have kids or a kid?" she asked, trying to keep the emotion out of her voice.

"Had. A daughter... She died at three weeks old. SIDS."

Pain coated his words, his deep timber suddenly heavier, and he swallowed, his gaze still on the road. Ava's heart dropped and immediately, uncontrollably tears welled in her eyes. The hum of the Christmas music was still circulating in the cab as she released a slow breath. She couldn't burst into tears like a weirdo and make the situation even worse but she wanted to.

"I'm so sorry, Elias." Her voice was quiet, restrained when she finally trusted herself enough to speak.

He twisted his lips, releasing a breath, when she passed him the thermos, her fingers brushing his. He accepted it, taking a sip of the hot chocolate, with one hand on the wheel. The gesture was as natural as it was intimate and Elias' eyes said he felt the same when he looked at her again. The energy shift in the cab was palpable. It charged before, with the physical pull they had but now, the connection felt emotional. She could only imagine what losing a child was like. How do you ever mover past that? What kind of strain does that put on—

"We didn't work out," Elias offered, already in tune with her thoughts again. "Her mom and I. After that we just...fell apart." He shook his head. "It was rough."

"How long were you together?"

"Five years. We stayed together for one after we lost the baby."

"I bet that put a lot of stress on your relationship," Ava offered aloud, biting the inside of her lip.

"It did," Elias admitted, glancing her way. He squinted at the night road. "People always talk about there being a reason for everything."

"I think that's bullshit," Ava interjected quietly.

Elias briefly met her eyes. "Exactly. I still haven't figured out the reason for something like that. Drove myself crazy trying to figure one out."

He shook his head, his eyes faraway.

"You know I kept buying stuff for her? For six months after we lost her, I just kept buying little things. Pacifiers, baby bottles, lotion, almost every time I went to the store, I'd just find myself in the baby aisle, like a... compulsion."

Ava bit the inside of her lip, studying his profile. His gaze was heavy when he glanced at her, almost as if he was expecting judgment.

"Finally, one day it just clicked, that she wasn't here and I had to move on." He paused, pulling in a breath, his eyes on the blackened, snow-filled sky. "Some things just are. And you just gotta learn to deal. Either that or succumb."

Ava leaned her head back against the seat cushion, expelling a breath. She turned her hand up on the seat between them and he placed his in hers, drawing a line across her palm unseeingly with his rough fingertips. Like he was soothing *her* after having told her something so heavy. He looked over at her and smiled, their eyes locking for a weighty second before he returned his attention to the road.

"Yo, I take it back," Elias said after a few long seconds of them both remaining quiet, lost in their separate thoughts, as he rubbed the pad of his thumb absently over her wrist. "*This* is the best Christmas jam ever."

He released her hand and reached to turn up the radio, bobbing his head. Ava laughed, though she regretted the loss of contact, slight as it was.

"You can't be serious. 'I Saw Mama Kissing Santa Claus?'" Ava asked wide-eyed, willing to lighten up the mood and play along with him.

"It had all the elements of a classic—hurt feelings, infidelity, mama creepin', son snitchin' about what he saw goin' down in the living room..." He took a swallow from the thermos and passed it back to Ava.

"Um, you do realize that Santa was his *daddy*, Elias."

"Nah." Elias shook his head, his dimples peeking out,

making her tingle everywhere. "Mama was *creepin'* on Christmas."

"No, she *wasn't*."

"Yep, listen—" he inclined his head toward the radio and widened his eyes as a young Michael Jackson sang about mama kissing Santa under the mistletoe on the Jackson 5 record.

"I've heard the song a million times. Santa was his daddy."

Elias shook his head. "Nope, not buyin' it. She was creepin'."

"Whatever," Ava said, laughing as Elias dropped another sexy grin on her.

"Oh! I almost forgot," she exclaimed, digging into her purse and extracting the cookies she'd taken from her mom's house. "I have cookies for the hot chocolate."

She grinned and passed one to Elias.

"Wow," he said, around a mouthful of cookie a few seconds later. "You made these?"

"I wish. My mom did."

"Damn, I was about to propose if you told me you made these cookies, Ava."

"You'd marry me for a cookie?"

"For a cookie like this, hell yes. We could work out the rest."

Ava laughed, shaking her head as Elias dropped another half-grin on her as he chewed.

They were approaching town and Elias pulled off the exit, heading in the opposite direction of her mom's place, which was close to the small college where she taught, toward the affluent section of town.

"What do your parents do?"

"My dad is a retired army general and lawyer. My mom owns a couple of daycares in the area."

"Did you ever think about following your dad into the military? Or was photography always your thing?"

"Photography was always my thing. I just didn't know I could actually make a living from it. Didn't know anything about how to go about it. So, I enlisted in the army straight out of high school. It didn't work out." He pushed out a chuckle and shook his head.

"What?" Ava asked, reading his rueful expression. He glanced at her, biting the inside of his cheek as if debating on if he was going to continue.

"I ended up getting put out. Got caught with some weed," he admitted, grinning as he shook his head. Ava's eyes widened.

"What'd your dad say?"

"Nothin nice," Elias said, chuckling as he glanced at her. "I think he knew that that wasn't the life for me though, so he got over it... eventually."

"You really were a bad ass."

Elias grinned. "Took me a minute to find my lane."

"And now you're in it? Your lane?"

"Yep. I made my mistakes early. I'm glad I got that outta my system back then. Nothing worse than a grown ass man still wandering around, not knowing what he's here for."

"Ain't that the truth," she said, thinking of her own path. Her career was settled for the most part, but with men? Now that was a different story. "There's nothing worse than a person, man or woman, who doesn't know who they are. It's stressful, dealing with people like that."

Elias glanced at her. "Sounds like you have experience."

"My ex was a lot like that." She grinned and shook her head. She hadn't meant to blurt that information out. "He's an actor and I think trying on all of those different personalities and characteristics started messing with his brain. He was always searching for something, externally."

Elias glanced at her, and once more the words were leaving her lips, uninhibited.

"He's the lead love interest on the show *Angel Hunter*, about the black-girl superhero? It's on the network I work for."

"I know it's huge," Elias said, glancing at her before returning his attention to the road. "But I haven't really gotten into it yet," he admitted.

"It's a mostly female viewership," Ava said. "It was kind of an experiment to see how the network would do with a show based on super heroes, especially one who's a black female, but it's really taken off. Anyway, when things went south, it got pretty tough."

"Work relationships can get messy," Elias said knowingly.

"I was actually with him before he landed the show. I started at the network, and a couple of months later, he got the part. I never directly worked on *Angel Hunter* but... yeah. It was hard when we broke up."

"How long ago was that?"

"About three months ago."

Elias nodded, his eyes on the road. Ava bit the inside of her lip, wondering what on earth had possessed her to share all that information about Ty. She took a bite of her cookie, chewing silently as she looked out of the window.

"I almost got cut dating a co-worker back in the day," Elias told her after a few long seconds.

Ava smiled as she swallowed. "You broke her heart?"

"And she broke the windows out my car."

Ava's eyes widened and she covered her mouth with her

hand as she laughed. He chuckled along with her, shaking his head.

"Damn, player," she teased, her smile still wide.

"Nah, she ain't have to smash the windows out of my Acura, man. I liked that car. We weren't serious enough for all that drama."

He grinned and finished off his cookie, and Ava's gaze was drawn to his lips... again.

"The things that are often conveniently inconsequential for men, mean a lot more to women. Maybe your relationship with home girl didn't mean much to you but she was obviously really emotionally involved to get that violent."

"Sounds like your rationalizing crazy, Ava." His voice was warm and husky and she bit the inside of her lip as she met his brown eyes.

"I'm just offering an alternative perspective."

"Okay." He grinned, eyes still on the road.

"My situation was pretty rough, honestly," she admitted. "I didn't smash the windows out his car, though. And we were serious. Looking at wedding rings serious. Five years of my life serious."

She thought about the groupies she ignored as Ty shot to stardom as the show picked up. The late nights. The overlooking. The accommodating and adjusting and the bending she did to make their relationship work.

"We broke up because he got another woman pregnant. Now they're engaged."

She said the words quickly, in a rush to get them out and off her tongue, surprised again that she was blurting out info to this dude she didn't even know like that.

"I'm sorry that happened to you." His voice was low and comforting, like his eyes when he looked at her.

She forced a smile.

"Oh, the irony, right? I spent my entire early adult life trying to avoid a situation like my parents'... and yet..." She waved a hand over herself. "*Isn't it ironic?*" she sang, mimicking Alanis Morissette.

He grinned, and she smiled, shrugging. "But it's all life, right? Learn the lesson and keep it moving."

Elias smiled, his gaze turning thoughtful as he openly studied her.

"So, this dude. You over him?"

Ava jerked her head up at Elias' sudden inquiry, her brow creased in mild surprise at his directness.

"Yes."

He narrowed his eyes a bit as if she said it too hastily to be believable.

"These past few months let me breathe a little," she admitted. "I got to see how much we relied on our work to be the focal point of our relationship. But I think it's more the idea of failure that made me so upset about us being over. I spent a lot of time building that relationship, working on it. Always thinking that if I gave a little more, compromised a little more..." She stopped, looking out of the window. "And now, it's like, yes, I have the life lesson and all of that jazz but what about the *time*? Ya know?"

She looked at him again and Elias nodded, a slight smile on his face. "I feel you."

"It made it harder because everywhere I looked, there he was." She shrugged twisting her lips, as she looked down at her hands, thinking about the public pregnancy announcements on the blogs and websites, stories that she thankfully didn't have to work, but knifed her in the gut anyway.

"It woulda been easier if I didn't have a constant

reminder of my failure but..." she shrugged again. "It is what it is."

"*Your* failure?" Elias raised a brow, glancing at her.

"You know what I'm saying," she said dismissively. "Like I said, it is what it is."

Ava met his discerning gaze, before peering out of the window silently as they pulled further into town, noting that most of the businesses in the area thankfully had power.

A few minutes later, Elias was turning into a residential neighborhood, where the houses were large and heavily decorated, mostly with white lights because people tended to think they were classier. He pulled in front of a large brick house with bay windows, a huge wrap-around porch and a perfectly manicured lawn that was notable even through the snowfall.

"*Wow*. Your parents' home is *gorgeous.*"

"This is their retirement home, my mom's dream house," he grinned. "I remember my dad was having a fit because my mom insisted on five bedrooms, so we'd all have our own rooms. We moved into it my senior year, so by that time it was just me and Matthew at home. But she wanted it, and my dad's a sucker when it comes to my mom so..." He shrugged, grinning sexily again. Or maybe he just grinned regularly, but it was sexy because it was Elias.

"Did you just call your dad a 'sucker' for wanting to please his wife?"

He chuckled. "Nah, my parents have an ideal relationship. They've been married almost forty years, and they actually still like each other. No separate bedrooms, no silence. That's the worst thing that could happen I think... having a silent marriage."

He glanced at her as he pulled into the spacious garage,

and she nodded in agreement. A second later, he'd hopped out of the truck, grabbed her luggage, and was opening her door. She slid out, taking a deep breath as he closed the door behind her. The garage was cold but very clean. Another vehicle that Ava assumed was his mom's was parked next to the truck, and a large work bench sat along the far wall next to a neat stack of boxes. It didn't even smell like a garage or motor oil. In fact, Ava didn't think she'd ever seen a garage that was so immaculate. She sucked in a quiet breath, suddenly nervous, which was ridiculous.

Elias was watching her.

"You okay?" He pulled off his skull cap, running his fingers over his head. His hair was grown out a little, but still low enough for it to be straight, just before it would curl.

Ava shifted her weight and nodded. She almost felt as if she was meeting a boy's parents on her first date.

"I'm fine," she finally responded.

He quirked a brow, waiting for her to speak. It was crazy how well he already seemed to know her, to be able to gauge her mood.

"It's just that I'm about to impose on your family, Elias, and it's weird. And it's Christmas. And I'm all like, 'Hey, Elias family! Your son barely knows me, we just met at a Christmas party like, two-point-five seconds ago before I made him rescue me from the side of a literal ditch, but Merry Christmas! I'm sleeping on your couch now!'"

Elias laughed, a deep rumbling sound that filled the confines of the garage, his eyes crinkling at the corners. He finally shook his head, a smile still on his lips, staring at her as if she were the cutest thing he'd seen in a while. He stepped closer, sitting her luggage on the ground. Her back pressed against the side of the truck and she inhaled at his sudden nearness.

"Ava, I told you I got you. Okay?" He waited until she met his dark brown eyes. "No one is tripping, and we have the room. And I'd never put you on the couch. You can have my bed."

She was watching his lips move and she blinked, trying to focus.

"You'd give me your bedroom?"

He chuckled. "I'm a thirty-four-year-old man, Ava. I don't have a 'bedroom' at my parent's house. But, yes. You can have the bed I sleep in when I'm here."

"I can't let you—" she started, and he rolled his eyes.

"Let's not go through this whole thing, alright?"

"What whole thing?" She blinked, staring at him indignantly.

He grinned and stepped a little closer to her, crowding her personal breathing space.

"The thing where you fight me on silly shit, like taking my bed. We both know that's what's gonna end up happening because one, you're my guest..."

"And two?" she asked, raising her brows, flirting with him.

The corner of his mouth quirked up and he stared into her eyes. "I'm a gentleman."

She smiled and looked down at the ground before meeting his eyes again.

"That you are," she admitted.

"And I dig you. A lot. So, I need for you to keep on liking me."

He'd stepped a little closer so that they were nearly touching, and she had to tilt her head up to meet his eyes.

"You keep saying I like you with a lot of confidence."

He grinned, though it reached his eyes more than his lips.

"Let's not do that either."

"What?"

The word came out far more breathlessly than she intended.

"The thing where you pretend like you're not feeling me too."

He had her by the bottom of the jacket, and she felt herself swaying closer, tempted to press upon her tip toes to press her lips to his. Because he was right; she *did* like him. Elias bit the corner of his lip, his gaze hot when it trailed to her mouth again.

"Elias," she said, her voice way breathier than she intended it for it to be.

"Ava."

His gaze was still fixed on her, and he tucked her hair behind her ear, his eyes low, as he let his fingertips graze her ear. Her eyes flitted closed and the warmth in her belly circled lower, gathering and pulsing.

"We should go inside," she said, opening her eyes.

He grinned, releasing a breath, his eyes turning thoughtful as he studied her, then nodded.

"You're right, we should," he said, extending his hand for her to take. "Come on."

SIX

He was caught up.

That's the only thing that could explain the past few hours, since he'd reconnected with Ava. Elias couldn't believe he'd gotten that deep with her in the car.

Since her death, he'd rarely talked about his daughter. Not to his mom, who gently tried to support him in the months following by getting him to talk, and still bought a Christmas ornament for Kayla every year, right along with Matthew's girls. Not to his brothers—who he chopped it up with all the time, about every and anything, but never seemed to have the words for when it came to losing Kayla. The conversations were all surface, because Elias couldn't bring himself to go beyond that. He couldn't bring himself to share the worst parts of what he was feeling. It felt as if he'd be lingering there, in that gut-wrenching place he'd been so desperate to escape so that he could function normally.

But he'd shared things he hadn't uttered aloud ever with Ava. Even Janay didn't know what he'd told Ava in the truck, about him still buying things for Kayla, months later. Talking to her had almost been like talking to himself. Like a stream of consciousness in a safe space of no judgment or expectation for the way he should feel.

That last year they were together, it was Janay's biggest complaint—he didn't talk. He was too closed off from her. He wouldn't "let her in." She didn't realize she was "in"—as much as any woman ever had been. That he just needed a minute, to get his head right, without feeling like he was somehow failing her, adding to her ever-present unhappiness. In the end, they were both so dispassionate about their relationship, each of them having already mentally detached, it didn't make much difference what he did anyway. The silence between them was deafening.

That he talked so easily with Ava, with no real explanation as to why that was, had him messed up. Everything with Ava was guttural. That's where he was feeling her, in his gut and chest, and nothing about it was rational.

In the garage earlier, he wanted so badly to press her up against that truck and just explore the chemistry between them—let it take them wherever it would in the moment. But she'd stopped him, not verbally, but with the look in her eyes, which he felt extended far beyond the moment with him. She'd been burned and she was cautious. It was all over her.

She was also feeling him. Her curiosity was all over her too, and he'd been tempted to just press her a little bit to see how much, or even if she'd resist him.

But after they left the garage, Elias made up his mind to back up off her a little. She was already staying over at his parents', which even though circumstantial, felt significant after that truck ride. But then she walked into the kitchen, won over his entire family in less than thirty minutes, and had him completely intrigued all over again.

None of the trepidation she'd expressed in the garage was present when Ava charmed his mom and dad as they lingered in the kitchen, having a nightcap but really, waiting up for him to get back. He understood how she excelled in public relations. She had a knack for making other people feel comfortable but even more than that, she had a way of turning the conversation to focus on the other person, and picking up instantly on the person's interests and strengths because she actually cared enough to pay attention.

She'd done it first with his mom, Hope, commenting on the décor of the house, intuitively recognizing that interior design was her hobby. Within a minute, his mom was telling Ava all about the design schemes at her daycares, which she'd taken care of herself.

Same with his dad. Ava commented on Joe's bourbon collection—chitchatting with him about his Kentucky roots, and joking with him about how Kentucky needed to be more like France. Only champagne from Champagne could be called "champagne"—everything else had to be sold as "sparkling wine." Bourbon was Kentucky grown but the state had yet to firmly associate itself with the liquor the way France had. Joe was impressed Ava knew all of that. *He* was impressed that she knew all of that.

He knew his mom wanted to press him for more information about Ava after meeting her, even though he'd explained how'd they reconnected at Kendrick's and their earlier history before he left to pick her up from that ditch. But she didn't because that wasn't Hope's style, especially after they all moved out and fell into adulthood.

After his parents headed to bed, Elias took her into the

den to meet his brothers. His mom insisted on a one-level house, so that as they aged, they wouldn't have to deal with stairs, and the den was on the far end of the house, separate from the master bedroom as possible.

Ava made short work of winning them all over as well. Even Daniel, who was perpetually pissed off because he'd just gone through a nasty divorce and was down on women, and life in general, thought she was alright. Elias knew his brothers were feeling Ava because now, only forty-five minutes after first meeting her, they were talking as if she weren't even there. Like she was just part of the fam. Apparently, the strange familiarity he felt with this woman extended even to his brothers, which had him a little shook.

He was standing at the small cherry wood bar, which he'd help install with Joe a few years back. Joe was the craftsman, but Elias helped him out enough years back while he was still trying to figure out what to do with himself, that he'd picked up some skill with wood too. The bar, which was now stacked mostly with bourbons, whiskeys, and rum, sat adjacent to the pool table. Elias focused on the crystal glasses he'd pulled out as he sprinkled a bit of cinnamon into the eggnog and rum drink for Ava, who was seated on one of the high back wooden barstools, her legs crossed under her.

"It *smells* like Christmas in here," she told him dreamily when they entered the spacious, airy house. Most of the cooking was finished already, and the scent of cinnamon and warm sugar lingered in the air, mingling with the rich cajun spices of the gumbo.

Ava was now wearing a pair of baggy red, fluffy Christmas pajamas that said "Get Lit" underneath a huge green Christmas tree. She'd gone back to the room, saying she needed to check in with her mom, and he thought she'd probably crash afterward. But she peeked her head around the entrance way to the den room wearing her PJs just twenty minutes later, asking if she could hang, much to Jeremiah and Matthew's amusement.

Elias looked up from the bar and met Ava's eyes again. They were the color of the sky right after the sun disappeared, not quite midnight black but visceral and appealing in their mysteriousness. She pressed her tongue against the inside of her cheek and gave him another one of her cute-ass half-smiles, which he'd been getting more and more often as the night wore on. The one that made his heart race a little bit and his groin tighten because he wanted to know this woman, and he knew it was all over him. *Yeah, he was definitely caught up.*

"Everything was good with your family?" he asked her, his voice low.

She nodded, tucking a strand of hair behind her ear. "They didn't get caught in the storm, thankfully. They're at the hospital now. Jeff's daughter is doing better than they initially thought, so that's good."

"Cool, glad everything is okay," he offered just as Matthew blurted, "You see this shit?"

"What?" Elias asked, reluctantly tearing his eyes away from Ava.

Matthew leaned his back against the large pool table that sat in the center of the den room and passed his phone to Jeremiah, his eyes now on Daniel who was preparing to try to hit the striped ball. Daniel looked tired to Elias, and not just because he'd just flown in from Dallas earlier. He was working non-stop, trying to get his mind off his failed marriage, no doubt.

"Wait..." Jeremiah's eyes widened and he turned the

phone sideways, his face scrunched. "Hell nah. Is that *Shay?*"

"*Yes.*" Matthew's eyes were wide when he looked at his older brother.

"The hell is she talkin' about, though?" Jeremiah asked, frowning as he held the phone toward Elias for him to get a look.

Ava gamely passed him the phone, a small smile on her lips, her eyes curious as she looked at him and his brothers.

"Shay is the cousin of a cousin of a cousin," Jeremiah explained as Elias looked at the picture and smirked, shaking his head, before handing it for Ava to check out. Her eyes widened and she grinned.

"At least she's being supportive?" Ava suggested, with a small shrug, passing the phone to Daniel, who accepted it from her with a grunt and eye roll, as Matthew took his shot on the pool table, loudly clacking the balls together, because he was terrible at pool.

"That's what's wrong with people," Matthew spoke up, scratching under his skull cap, his curly hair peeking from beneath it with his movement. "All this fake shit starts getting credence."

The picture was an ass shot of Shay, wearing a tiny bikini with her butt out, standing at a balcony staring out into the sky with a caption that read: "*As I look out into the distance, I think of all the brothers who are unjustly locked up because of this unfair system. My heart goes out to you all. #JustUs*"

Elias smirked and shook his head again. Shay was on one.

"Dayton is locked up, about to do *two years,* and this is the shit she has the gall to post?" Matthew asked, leaning on his pool stick. His eyes were still wide, as they were whenever he was animated, which was most of the time. His baby brother wore every emotion he ever felt right on his sleeve, for the world to see and judge. "That shit is *hella* disrespectful," he said.

"Dayton is the cousin of another cousin of another cousin," Jeremiah informed Ava.

"Ah. Got it," she said, nodding her head, still laughing as Jeremiah grinned exchanging a look with Elias. Matthew lived with him, but it was Jeremiah who probably knew Elias the best.

"Shay's been out here lost," Daniel said. His eyes were now on the pool table as he took another shot, on his way to what would make his third win in the past hour since they'd entered the room.

"Man, whatever," Matthew grumbled. "She needs to get found. You can't be out here using hashtags like it just don't mean anything; like corporate prisons ain't real and fools ain't out here gettin' locked up for nothin' on the daily. This dude is about to be on lock down for two years on some bullshit and you out here getting likes on Instagram. Fuck outta here."

He waved his hand dismissively.

"That's her thing now," Elias shrugged. "She's gettin' paid to use her page."

Elias handed Ava the egg nog and rum he'd made for her, and she accepted it with another smile, clearly enjoying the antics of his brothers.

"Thank you," she said, taking a sip and making another one of those faces like the one she'd made when he gave her the hot chocolate in the truck earlier. She smiled up at him again, and he bit the corner of his lip, allowing his gaze to rest on her mouth as she sipped the creamy liquid, catching a drop with her tongue when it threatened to drip down her chin.

"What'd they get Dayton on?" Daniel interjected, not looking up from the table as he perfectly shot the 8-ball into the pocket for the win.

"He was on probation, right?" Jeremiah asked, swallowing a gulp of beer before setting the bottle down on the bar and getting up to rack.

"For a gun and drug charge he caught *ten years* ago, dude," Matthew said, shaking his head, not even concerned that he'd lost, badly.

"And he was *still* on probation?" Jeremiah spoke up, brow furrowed.

"Prison is a business," Daniel supplied, watching as Jeremiah set up the table for another game.

"He got arrested for reckless driving or somethin' a couple of weeks back and it was a wrap," Matthew said. "Probation violation, two years. And now Shay wanna go posting her ass for everyone to see, pretending like she's holding him down."

"That is foul," Jeremiah conceded.

"In the future, when we look back on how we messed up the earth, I promise it's all gonna point back to social media," Matthew said.

"I agree," Ava bobbed her head up and down as she sipped on her drink.

"The downfall of civilization will be and has always been power-hungry men," Jeremiah argued, glancing in Matthew's then Ava's direction. "All social media does is put a spotlight on human weakness. That's it."

"So, power is weakness?" Matthew challenged Jeremiah, raising a brow.

"Anything that consumes you is weakness," Elias answered, swallowing his drink.

"I think social media *warps* human weakness, makes it worse *because* of that spotlight," Ava argued.

"Word." Matthew nodded, shooting Elias a look. Elias knew he was impressed with Ava and Matthew smiled when he looked at her again. "And didn't you say you work in social media?"

"Well, not exactly, really... I'm a publicist for a women's centered network," Ava corrected.

"But you deal with social media for the actors you represent, right?" Matthew cocked a brow at her and Ava lifted her shoulders.

"I mean, yeah, some."

"And most of the things you have to clean up as a publicist is because of something dumb someone said on social media, right?"

Ava scrunched her nose cutely, thinking.

"I did just have to craft a statement right before we went on holiday. One of the reality stars-turned-actors said 'Women should dress how they want to be addressed' and got dragged by feminist Twitter for 'purporting rape culture.' Then he got into it with some feminist writer and called her a 'bitch,' which was about the stupidest thing he could've done. I had to write a statement from the network saying we 'don't embrace those views'."

"Gerrard Smith?" Jeremiah questioned.

Ava nodded.

Matthew rolled his eyes, shaking his head. "He's a bum."

"It didn't help that he had a domestic violence charge from back when he was eighteen—I don't know who fished that out of the archives," Ava admitted, casting a glance in Elias' direction.

"That was some stupid shit to say," Jeremiah said.

"It was overblown," Matthew countered. "Dude is dumb for saying that silly shit out loud but they act like he actually sexually assaulted someone or something. Saying stupid shit can't be treated the same way as actually doing it."

"They did kinda take it the next level," Ava agreed. "So yeah," she said, turning toward Matthew, grinning, "long story short, cleaning up after people on social is the worst. I get a little break because I don't represent the talent directly. But the little bit I have to do with the network, and working with the talent's personal publicists can be such a drag. I hate social media."

Ava sipped from her drink, furrowing her brow, reminding Elias of their earlier conversation when she said she wanted to switch gears professionally.

"That's why I detached," Daniel spoke up. "I don't even miss it."

"All it is, is a bunch of depressing headlines and people pretending like they know shit, then arguing over stupid shit, like whether sugar or salt is better on grits... like, are you serious right now?" Matthew questioned, as Elias laughed.

"But I can't front, I be on that shit... like all the time," Matthew laughed. "Shit's addictive," he admitted.

Matthew grinned, then perched next to Ava on the seat Jeremiah had just occupied.

"Did E show you his film?" Matthew asked Ava, tossing Elias a look before fixing his attention on Ava again.

"His *film*?" she repeated, eyes wide.

"Yeah," Matthew continued. "He co-wrote and directed

a short film about exactly that. Social media's impact on black middle school kids."

Ava whipped her head to look at him and Elias stared at Matthew, who returned his look without blinking. Elias' boy Sean worked in Atlanta Public Schools and wanted Elias' help in putting together a short film to present to the district about effects of social media on young people. It was Sean's project, Elias only had the resources to help make it happen. But the more involved he got with the project, the more fascinated he became, on more than just an artistic level.

Ava was still staring at him with round eyes and Elias shook his head, taking another healthy swig of his bourbon and eggnog. Matthew whipped out his phone, leaning in close so Ava, who peered at it, could see the screen.

"This is just the trailer," Matthew explained before he started it.

"I can't believe you're a filmmaker," she said, turning to look at him again.

"I'm not a filmmaker."

"But you made a film," Ava challenged, cocking her head to the side, daring him not to grin at her. He failed.

"I had the downtime and the resources, and I helped put together a little project for my boy," he corrected.

"That kinda sounds like complete crap, Elias. You made a film, and you are therefore a filmmaker."

She looked at him pointedly, then made a show of staring at Matthew's phone. Elias chuckled and took another swig of his drink, ignoring Jeremiah's knowing smirk from across the room when he glanced up at him.

"Wow," Ava breathed, after a few seconds of staring at Matthew's screen.

"*Elias.*" Her eyes went round again. "I can't believe you. Where'd you even get the idea for this?"

"My friend Sean teaches eighth grade English. He wanted to document the physical and emotional effects of social media on them. I had the time and the resources, and I helped him out."

"But you co-wrote and directed it?"

"Turned out to be more interesting than I thought," he shrugged.

Ava was staring at him in wide-eyed disbelief. Elias downed the last of his drink before pouring himself another, this one bourbon without the eggnog.

"Well, the trailer is *incredible*. Have you shown the film to anyone entered any short film festivals or...?"

"We weren't even thinking like that, to be real. It was a project for his work—that's it."

"I could help you, you know. I can help you figure it out if you're interested in getting it out there. This is my lane."

She met his eyes directly, arching a brow, daring him to deny her as if that were something he actually wanted to do.

"We'll see what's up," he acquiesced, earning him a small satisfied smile.

"How was the Christmas party?" Matthew asked, looking at Elias.

"It was aight," he grinned a little when he met Ava's eyes. "You shoulda came."

"Nah, I was cool on that."

Elias shook his head and Daniel rolled his eyes, exchanging a glance with Jeremiah. Matthew and their cousin Kendrick stayed into it. Elias couldn't even remember what they were beefin' about this go around.

Matthew's phone buzzed in his hand and he frowned, muttering a low curse.

"What's up with you?" Jeremiah asked, looking up from the pool table.

"Zoe."

Matthew said it almost like a curse, and Elias exchanged a glance with Jeremiah, who'd stuffed his hands in his pockets, watching their baby brother as he slid off the stool and paced in front of the couch, which was pushed against the far wall, opposite of the pool table. Daniel looked up at him too, and rolled his eyes before fixing his attention on the pool table once more, taking careful aim for his next shot.

"You know I'm supposed to have the girls tomorrow, but she started tripping at the last minute." Matthew shook his head, pulling at his skull cap. "Zoe thinks she's hurting me by doing this kind of shit, but she's hurting *them*."

Matthew and the mother of his children, Zoe, had been off and on for almost eight years, since Matthew was nineteen, and his first daughter, Noelle was born. And in all that time—even after having *another* baby, an adorable little girl, Brielle, who was now two— they hadn't been able to get it together.

"How is she keepin' them from you? Ain't they already at her mom's?" Daniel asked, watching as Matthew continued pacing. Zoe's parents lived a few blocks away.

Matthew nodded tightly, still scowling. "She says she's coming over here with them tomorrow. Like she's suddenly worried about me keeping my own damn kids."

"More like she's worried about Meghan being here," Elias offered dryly, eyeing his brother.

Matthew shot him a look and shook his head. Meghan was Matthew's on-and-off again girlfriend. He brought her around occasionally, using the girl as a pawn because, really, everyone knew he wanted Zoe. And their back and forth tug-of-war wasn't about the girls but *them*. Matthew was spoiled and temperamental, and so was Zoe. The result of those two personalities clashing was often disastrous, even reckless, considering they had two other little people they'd created to think about now.

"Man, let all that go for the night," Daniel said, leaning against the table while Jeremiah took his shot. "Enjoy your babies on Christmas and chill on all that drama you and Zoe constantly got goin' on for once."

Matthew rolled his eyes, hitting a button on his phone.

"Zoe, why you do this shit?" he answered. He glanced up and threw two fingers in the air.

"Good night," he said, ambling out of the room, talking to Zoe in low tones.

"Merry Christmas, Zo-Zo," Jeremiah called out, chuckling, exchanging a look with Daniel.

"I thought they had the custody stuff worked out," Daniel said, turning to look at Elias.

Elias shrugged. "They're at the house all the time. Things seemed cool."

"Matthew likes drama. So does Zoe," Jeremiah offered, taking another swig of his beer.

Daniel shook his head. "They're gonna mess up the girls if they don't get that shit together."

"Damn, I forgot their presents are still in the closet," Elias suddenly remembered.

He thought about just not wrapping the gifts, like last year, and just letting them pull the stuff out of the department store bags. But he didn't feel like hearing his mom's mouth about how he was messing up Christmas by being tacky, and the girls did seem to get super geeked about unwrapping things.

"Hey," Elias said, pulling lightly at the back of Ava's fluffy red pajama shirt. The bar counter was still separating them, and she turned to look up at him. "I gotta go wrap presents. Wanna come with me? Let me put you to work?"

Ava smiled, those midnight eyes of her mischievous. "You wanna put me to work?" She cocked her head a little, eyeing him.

"You down?" he asked his voice low. "Or you too tired?"

"I'm never too tired," she countered, meeting his eyes.

He chuckled. *He was definitely caught up.*

SEVEN

"Thinking about you. Heard it was bad out that way... how are you?"

Ava blinked at her phone and re-read the message, just to make sure that it was Ty, sending a casual text message on Christmas Eve as if they yucked up all the time since he'd broken her heart and smeared his cheating-ass semen into another woman. *Was he serious?*

She glared at the message for another second, heart pounding, before stuffing her phone into her oversized pajama pocket and taking a long sip of the egg nog and whiskey mix Elias made her before they left the den.

Ty was crazy. And disrespectful. Wasn't Trinity four months pregnant now? Shouldn't he be tending to his fiancé with a gut full of baby instead of worrying about her? And why did he just assume that she was in Macon and not in Atlanta?

Because he was supposed to be out here with you, dummy.

Ava took a deep breath, upset with herself for being so affected by Ty's stupid text, as Elias rounded the corner into the airy living room from the hallway with a huge department bag in his hand. He grinned at her when their gazes connected, and she smiled back automatically.

She'd stopped trying to analyze why Elias affected her so thoroughly about an hour ago. It just *was*. The magnetic pull he had on her seemed natural, unforced. That was the difference between Elias and Ty. Elias was comfortable in his skin, in the way that only grown men were. Ty was confident but still reaching for outside validation in too many areas of his life.

"You straight?" Elias asked as she hovered in front of the plush couch.

"I'm good." She smiled again and nodded, sipping her drink, which was delicious. When he told her he'd bartended for a few years, she wasn't surprised. There didn't seem to be much he *hadn't* done.

What had shocked her a little bit though, was how gorgeous his brothers were. Usually, there was only one, *maybe* two extremely good looking siblings in a family. Elias had one of those slots covered for sure. But every single one of his brothers looked like they could star in a television series.

Her brain automatically ran through the scenarios for a drama starring the Young men. She couldn't help it—working in television for the past five years kind of made it an automatic whenever she went anywhere or met anyone interesting.

Matthew with his charming, free-spirited nature, toffee-colored eyes and curly hair that he didn't care to comb would be the emotional draw, the Young brother women wanted to take care of while he figured himself out. All he'd have to do was smile and they've be won over. He was emo in a way that leaned more toward passionate instead of sensitive, with a bit of a rough edge that tempered his almost pretty boy looks.

Jeremiah and Daniel were identical twins—which was really enough in and of itself. Jeremiah with his full beard, lithe football player build, and dark cocoa complexion would be the inadvertent playboy; the guy who didn't mean to break women's hearts because he'd be honest with them but would anyway because every woman he ever dated would want to make a life with him, in spite of his whimsical interests. Daniel was the most reserved of all of them, but had obviously been burned because his dark brown eyes differed from his twin's in that they were cool and assessing when he looked at her, like he was always trying to figure out a person's angle— especially if the person happened to have a vagina. He'd be the one women would want to fix and heal.

And Elias would be the wild card. The ruggedly handsome Young brother women tried to figure out because he adapted so seamlessly to every situation and showed a different side of his personality, depending on the environment. He went from flirtatious and charming to thoughtful and vulnerable to chilled and observant without ever feeling like he was forcing anything. And Ava was feeling every single one of his slight demeanor shifts. She was feeling *him*.

Elias walked barefoot across the spacious living room area with his bag of presents and slid down onto the floor in front the plush, eggshell leather couch where she was seated on the edge of the cushion. He'd changed into a pair of grey sweats and a white t-shirt that showed off his strong forearms, and her gaze lingered there before dipping downward over his flat abs. Even the man's feet were sexy. He caught her staring, awareness glinting in his dark brown eyes as he grinned slightly, and she felt her entire body heat.

"You only have two nieces, right?" Ava asked, tearing her eyes away from him and staring at the enormous bag he'd sat next to her feet.

"Yep, Matthew's girls, Brielle and Noelle."

The bag seemed to be glowing beneath the vibrant white lights from the huge Christmas tree that loomed just a few feet away. Elias' mom's decorating skills extended to her Christmas décor, which was just breathtaking, even in its simplicity. The tree was no different though monstrous in size, it wasn't off-putting, didn't feel like they were smack dab in the Macy's or something. It made the room feel cozy and warm.

Or maybe that was the fireplace that was softly flickering, just to her left. Or maybe it was the liquor in the delicious eggnog drink she couldn't seem to get enough of. Or maybe it was the way Elias was looking at her now. Like he wanted to find out how *she* tasted.

"How old are they again?" Ava asked, mostly as a distraction from his penetrating gaze, sipping from her egg nog once more as she slid down onto the floor next to him. Ignoring him, and the connection that was dancing between them was a challenge at this point. One she wasn't winning, especially with him so close and smelling so good, like laundry detergent and warmth and *man*.

"They're two and eight," Elias said, watching as she finally broke his gaze to pull a doll dressed like a "rock star" out of the bag. She peered into again, and smiled, shaking her head.

"What?" he asked, pulling out a pink and purple train set with glitter on the wheels.

"You're like Father Christmas with all these toys."

"I'm *Unc*," he said, grinning. "I'm supposed to spoil them."

"But they have two other uncles."

"And I'm their favorite. Gotta keep my status."

Ava laughed, her gaze dropping to Elias' full lips as he grinned.

"They're cool girls though. Super smart with their own little personalities," he said, taking a small hit of his whiskey. "So, that makes it easier to spoil them."

"Matthew lives with you right?"

He nodded. "He's been living with me for about year now. They're over the house a lot."

Ava watched as he wrapped the doll, not taking care to line up the corners or make the bright red and gold paper even before he taped it down. Over the past hour, he'd been quieter than before, not quite distracted, but not fully present either. But when he looked at her, it was like he came back again, offering one of his half-grins, giving her that look that made it feel as if her heart was fluttering in her belly.

Elias' phone buzzed in his sweat pocket and he pulled it out, staring at it for a second before dropping it next to him. His expression didn't change but she did notice, just barely, that he pushed out a breath before taking another healthy swallow of his whiskey. She took another sip of her own drink, enjoying the pleasant heaviness of the liquor, chastising herself internally for being worried about who was on his phone this late. She'd known the man for all of five hours.

"There's like, an entire environment happening in here," she said, smiling as she nodded toward the fireplace then the stereo, which was playing a Christmas Eve soul set.

Ron Isley was singing "Have Yourself A Merry Little Christmas."

Elias chuckled, his baritone low. "An environment?"

She smiled and he shook his head a little, refocusing on the gift he was wrapping. He fell silent again for a few long minutes.

She glanced at him, literally biting her tongue to keep from asking Elias if he was alright. It was one of the things that bugged Ty, that she was always trying to get into his head, change his mood. *"Just let me be sometimes, Ava,"* he'd say, exasperated. *"Stop trying to fix me."*

"This is such a great book," she said, picking up a copy of Jason Reynold's *Ghost* and running her fingertips over it.

"Dude is talented."

"You said your niece is only eight though, right?" She eyed him, a slight grin on her face and he chuckled.

"I know it's a little advanced for her but Matthew and Zoe let her watch those soap operas that come on the Disney Channel all the time. She's reading at a sixth-grade level—I think she can handle it. And I'd rather for her to be reading than being brainwashed by that goofy shit on Disney."

"I can definitely dig it. Reading is fundamental."

"Alright, Lavar Burton."

She laughed at his *Reading Rainbow* quip. "Shut up, Elias. For real though. *Reading Rainbow* was my show. I was a nerdy kid," she said shrugging when he widened his eyes and looked at her. "Reading was my absolute favorite past time, aside from watching basketball. I got it honestly. My mom's an English professor."

"You ever think about writing?" he asked, his eyes curious under the light of the fireplace. She shook her head.

"I love like... storytelling. But I'm not a great writer."

"Reading was my thing too, even when I was wildin' out. Stephen King, Zora Neale Hurston, James Baldwin, got really into Chuck Palahniuk for a minute."

"Fight Club is classic," Ava said grinning. "But I never read the book."

"You should, it's—"

"Always better than the movie," she finished for him.

"Although that's one where it might be running neck and neck. I had a big Cormack McCarthy phase too."

Ava grinned, remembering their earlier conversation, and how effortlessly he'd quoted *The Road*.

"You were all over the place," she said, looking up at him through her lashes, as she absently thumbed through the book.

"I just like good shit," he said, haphazardly taping the corner of a box. "If it's dope, I roll with it. Being confined to just one thing— that's never been me."

Ava twisted her lips. She was the exact opposite. Stability made her feel safe. She would try new things but only after she analyzed it thoroughly and was comfortable.

"You should sign this," she said, passing the book to him, her fingertips lightly brushing against his. She grabbed a pen off the floor next to the scissors.

He grinned but followed her suggestion, writing in strong lines inside the book cover before passing the book back to her. Ava immediately opened it, running a finger over the ink as she read.

"During your life, never stop dreaming. No one can take away your dreams." —Tupac Shakur

"You *are* the cool uncle, quoting 'Pac."

"You're kinda nosy, Ava," Elias teased, glancing up at her.

"Shut up."

He laughed. "She doesn't even know who Pac is for real anyway. He's just some old dead dude who took pictures with his shirt off and wore bandanas all the time."

Ava smiled.

"But I'mma teach her."

"Has your niece seen your short film then, since it's focused on middle school kids?"

He shook his head. "Nah. No one has really. It wasn't even about all that. Just a project to help out my boy."

"That didn't look amateur, though, Elias," she pressed. Ordinarily, she wouldn't push so hard, especially from someone so clearly reluctant. But his trailer was incredibly impressive. *He* was incredibly impressive. And she was beyond curious to view the project in its entirety. "I wanna see it."

"Okay," he said.

She tilted her head and stared at him. "For real."

"Okay," he repeated, still smirking, his tone too flat for her to take seriously.

She dropped it, though, and picked up her drink and took a sip. A few seconds later, she couldn't help but look at Elias again, discreetly studying his handsome profile as she wrapped a doll with an abnormally large head. He had a small slash on his right eyebrow, like maybe he'd gotten to a fight and it left a scar. His beard was just a little rougher than it'd been even a few hours ago. His eyelids were a bit lower, making his thick eyelashes seem longer. And his lips —they were masculine but full. He was squinting, biting the bottom corner of his lip as he wrapped presents, something Ava noticed he did when he seemed to be in deep thought.

Ava's gaze dropped from his face to his bicep, noting the tip of the tattoo stretching just beneath his t-shirt sleeve, able to make out that it said "Kayla" in beautiful script. He noticed her gaze on his tat and he grinned slightly, though it didn't reach his eyes. She knew it had to be tough, wrapping Christmas gifts for his littlest niece, who was just about as old as Kayla would've been now.

He finished wrapping the last gift and she smiled, watching as he moved toward the large tree, shoving them beneath it.

"Dude, not like that." She shook her head at the mess he was making, shooing him away as she arranged the presents beneath the tree neatly.

When she finished, she turned to see Elias still sitting on the floor, resting his back comfortably against the couch, watching her. Instantly, her entire body heated. That look in his eyes was... disconcerting. Arousing.

"Come'ere," he said, his deep voice quiet, playing against the soft backdrop of the music.

Ava made her way back to the couch, sitting with her back against it as well. There was still a couple of feet between them and Elias looked at her.

"Closer."

His eyes were hooded, the slight grin on his face beckoning. She hesitated for a second before scooting herself along the plush carpet, so that their shoulders were nearly touching.

"Better?"

"Almost." His dark brown eyes were teasing and his gaze raked over her features. "I appreciate your help with the gifts."

"I appreciate *your* help with... everything."

"I told you that ditch was a win for me."

She rolled her eyes and laughed. Elias grinned and ran a hand over the back of his neck, releasing a short yawn, which made his chest expand.

"You're tired. I should g—"

"Nah," he interrupted. His eyes were low. "Chill out with me for a minute. Unless you're too sleepy to hang?"

She shook her head, probably way too quickly. "I'm a night owl, honestly."

"Me too." He grinned at her.

"What?" She asked when he kept looking at her.

"You really are *pretty*, Ava." She was blushing, again.

"You really are charming, Elias."

He grinned, narrowing his eyes as he chewed on the inside of his lip.

"You keep sayin' that like it's a bad thing."

"It could be perceived as disingenuous."

He arched a brow, still smirking. "You think I'm 'disingenuous' now?"

"No."

"Good. Because that'd say more about you and your inability to take compliments than me."

"You have a smart-ass mouth, Elias."

"I'm sorry," he said, his deep tone playful.

"No, you're not."

"You're right. I'm not. I don't even know what the hell we're talkin' about right now."

She laughed, tilting her head back and covering her mouth to contain the noise. She dropped her hand and shook her head, still smiling.

Elias stared at her for a second, a small grin on his lips. He absently scratched the "Kayla" tattoo she'd admired earlier.

"This is beautiful." Her voice was soft. She reached and ran her fingers over Elias' warm skin, grazing the tat.

"Daniel did it for me about a year ago."

"He's a tattoo artist?"

"Nah," Elias shook his head as Ava continued tracing her fingers over the curved lines, noting the chill bumps that dotted his skin as she did so, and the desire in her lower belly tightened into a dull ache. He met her gaze, his deep brown eyes seeming to peer through her, and her pulse sped up even more. "He used to do tattoos here and there back when he was in college. I brought him out of retirement."

"Well, this is amazing," she said, her fingers still tracing the swirling lines. "It's so detailed and intricate."

"You got any ink?" he asked, grinning at her when she finally dropped her hand from his arm.

"One tattoo," she managed. "The required college-era lower back tat."

Elias chuckled, his warm timber deep and relaxed.

"A butterfly?" His eyes were dancing with amusement and something just beneath the surface that made the ache in her lower belly increase.

Ava shook her head, burying her face in her hands as she laughed. "I am so cliché."

He smiled, tilting his head up. "Lemme see."

Ava eyed him for a minute, trying not to smile at his alluring half-grin, before pushing the roll of unused paper aside and getting onto her knees next to him. She lifted her fluffy pajama shirt to just below her belly button and Elias leaned over to inspect the tattoo she'd gotten from a guy named Nasir who frequented Clark Atlanta's campus, looking for goofy girls to give predictable tattoos to. He was so close she could feel his breath warm against her back, and her heart rate doubled as she inhaled his clean, masculine scent, trying to regulate her breathing.

"This is actually good work," he said, his voice low as his rough fingers grazed the silver-dollar-sized butterfly that rested just below her waistline, setting her already warm skin on fire.

"Thank God. I couldn't have a lower back tat *and* have it be ugly," she managed, licking her lips. He was still tracing the lines his rough fingers, and she exhaled, struggling not to melt into his touch.

"Ava."

"Elias."

"Spend New Year's Eve with me."

His fingers dipped, tracing the wings of the butterfly, his invitation coming from nowhere.

"Where'd that come from?" she asked aloud.

"Me." There were traces of amusement in his voice. It felt as if he moved closer to her. The air shifted, became dense, and Ava inhaled when his fingertips trailed further up her back, tracing her spine. Her eyes fluttered closed.

"I have a little get together every year at the house," he explained, his voice low. "We do it low-key, just chill and hang out. I want you to be there."

She released a breath, shaking her head. She knew she was supposed to be resisting him but couldn't quite remember the exact details of why, not with him so close, smelling so good, his body emitting masculine energy that affected and charged every cell inside of her.

"I don't think..."

She turned, looking over her shoulder at him. He sat upright, their gazes connected, his hot and intense, despite the slight grin on his face.

"You don't think what?"

"I mean," she shook her head, glancing toward the fireplace.

"You mean?" he prompted, tilting his head.

"I'm not really looking to like, get involved or... start anything."

He smiled as if she was adorable.

"I just want more time with you, Ava." He said it simply, as if she was silly for putting up a fuss.

"You have more time with me now."

"I want more." His baritone was quiet. He reached, pulling lightly on the bottom hem of her shirt.

She turned her head, meeting his eyes, their lips only centimeters apart now. She could feel his warm breath against her lips, dizzying and intoxicating.

"You comin?" he asked, offering her a teasing grin, his eyes hooded even under the light of the fire place.

"Will you let me see your entire film?"

His smile increased, and he tugged again at the hem of her pajama shirt, willing her even closer.

"I'll let you see whatever you want, Ava," he said low against her ear, pressing a kiss to her temple, then just below her earlobe. Her skin was on fire, and her eyes fluttered closed as she sucked in a quick breath at the feel of his warm lips on her.

She should move away.

Another soft kiss on the side of her chin.

Move away from him, Ava.

Another one on her neck.

Move.

And she did. She turned her head and met his lips. A rush of air escaped her, and when she inhaled, it was all Elias. His kiss was hungry but controlled, like he didn't want her to be scared away but also as if he'd been waiting for this moment all night.

He pulled her bottom lip between his first, before kissing her top lip. She drew in a breath, her head swimming with Elias' masculine scent, when she finally opened for him.

He slid his warm tongue into her mouth then, stroking hers in a languid rhythm. He made a noise from deep in his chest, when a soft noise left her lips, pulling her closer by her shirt, his thumb making slow circles on her lower abdomen.

She was lost. Her body felt liquid, molten. Her thoughts floating and swirling away from her, and she was unable to grasp anything but the almost dream-like attraction she felt to Elias.

Whatever mental battle she was fighting with herself to resist Elias was shot, as the kiss picked up pace, Elias' facial hair scratching against her skin as their tongues tangled in an erotic, staccato rhythm.

This wasn't a good idea. Wasn't smart. Wasn't her. But she turned in his muscular arms at his urging, kicking the long forgotten wrapping paper across the plush carpet as she straddled him. He pulled at her hip with one hand, while the other cupped the back of her head, his fingers threading through her hair as he pressed her more firmly against his mouth.

There were few things more sensual than a kiss. The intimacy. The prelude to more. The way it could be aggressive, or slow and sensual, sweet or hungry and fierce. Ava didn't have a lot of sex in college- only with her boyfriend, Damon, who she lost her virginity to senior year. They were together for a couple of years and then, months after they split, she met and became consumed with Ty.

So, she didn't know sex with a lot of men, but she knew the sensuality of a kiss. And she knew that Elias, after only a few minutes in his arms, was the best she'd ever experienced. Because that's what she was doing—experiencing him. His light then heavy touches. The way he breathed against her mouth and tasted of whiskey and traces of cinnamon. The low sounds that left his chest, the weight of his breathing. Her skin was memorizing his touches.

Elias kissed in cadence with his personality shifts. One second, it was slow and leisurely, his tongue playfully dipping in and out of her mouth the next, it was hungry and aggressive, his fingers tugging lightly at her hair as he bit on her lower lip.

Elias pulled at her thighs again, and she instinctively rolled her hips against his erection, a low hum escaping her lips, matching the deep sound that left his muscled chest, even though there were still layers of clothes between them.

The kiss was turning feverish, electric, as she rocked on him, her fingers trailing over the hard planes of his chest, when she pushed her fingers beneath his cotton t-shirt in an effort to reach his skin.

In the back of her mind, she was trying to process what was happening, how it was that Elias kissed her like he *knew* her. He reached, cupping her face, letting his hands slide down her neck, his kiss hungry as he took control once more, his warm tongue demanding as it swept against hers.

She was grinding against him now, wantonly, like she'd lost her mind because she kind of had.

God, what was she doing?

She'd only met this man tonight— in spite of their high school connection. She was in his *parent's house*. She'd never in her thirty-one years had a one night stand, or come close to one. But she wanted Elias. And it was spurring and igniting everything inside of her as she melted into his kiss again, loving the way he was tugging lightly at her hair, as he swept his tongue against hers.

A burst of laughter from either Daniel or Jeremiah

suddenly floated down the hallway from the den, and Ava stopped abruptly, the air leaving her lungs in short, heavy spurts as she pressed her forehead against Elias'. She pulled back slightly and met his dark brown eyes, wetting her lips, tasting him there, wanting more. He grinned a little, seemingly unsurprised by the intensity of their chemistry. But his gaze never wavered from hers and she could make out the tiny specs of amber in his, as he stared at her, chest rising and falling quickly, waiting for her to decide how far they were going to take this.

Ava climbed off his lap, chest still heaving and looked off toward the flickering fireplace, straightening her pajamas. She touched her tongue to the corner of her mouth, unsurprised to find that Elias was still watching her. Their gazes linked again, and Ava swallowed, heading toward the bedroom.

Elias stood and followed her.

EIGHT

He was caught up.

Buried so deep inside Ava the only thing he could feel was her — warm and tight, her body naturally pulsing in rhythm to his movements.

She smelled faintly of baby lotion and something else that was succulent but subtle and made him want to bury his nose in her smooth skin. He reached up and ran his fingertips over her features, from her forehead to her soft lips, and she sucked the tip of his thumb into her mouth. *Shit.* Instantly, he swelled inside her even more.

When he first slid inside her, the way she gasped and stared up at him, her tightness, made him think it'd been a minute for her. Ava's midnight-colored eyes were translucent now when she met his gaze, her lips slightly parted, her accelerated breaths making her ample breasts rise and fall in a tempting rhythm. So, he lifted his head, capturing a hardened nipple between his lips, rolling it against his tongue, suckling harder when Ava moaned, her head falling forward so that her chin brushed the top his head as she wrapped her arms around his neck, drawing him closer, continuing the intoxicating rhythm of her hips.

The room was dark, save for the tiny, battery-operated decorative Christmas tree that was on the dresser across the room, and it almost appeared as if Ava was glowing beneath its yellow lights when he released her nipple. She met his eyes again before she slid back down against his chest, and he could feel the staccato beat of her heart beat against his sternum as she pressed her lips to his, kissing him slowly, sweetly, without regard for her transparency, without pretense.

He wanted Ava from the first second he saw her earlier tonight at Kendrick's. Before that even. And now? He was buried inside of her, and it still wasn't enough.

Elias wrapped his arms around her and turned his head, kissing and licking her jaw then her neck, dipping his head against her collar-bone, a deep noise leaving his chest, then slid both hands over her ass, squeezing her cheeks, pulling her soft curves more tightly against him.

She was slick and damp with sweat, her silky skin gliding over as she undulated her hips in a loose, erotic rhythm. Ava opened her eyes and looked at him as she kissed him, sucking on his lower lip like she couldn't get enough of the way he tasted either. He ran his hands up her upper thighs, flipping them so that he was on top because he was too close to coming, just off the energy between them when she kissed him like that.

His thrusts were fast and deep, his fingers buried in her soft curls, and Ava made another series of soft, silky noises from deep in her throat as she opened for him, grabbing at his lower back, then his ass, pulling him closer, tilting her head up to receive his kiss, arching her hips to match his rhythm. He grunted, closing his eyes briefly because she felt *so good. So good.*

Elias realized fleetingly that he was kissing her like they were in love, and Ava was responding to him like she was *his*. He was eerily present with her, in this moment, feeling everything. His thoughts were everywhere and nowhere, focused and hazy because they were both clinging and cascading on the woman beneath him, the cushion of her brown thighs, her soft breasts pressed against his bare chest, her heavy breaths, and the way she kept wanting him to be closer and closer, hooking her heels into his upper thighs, lifting her head to meet his mouth when their lips weren't touching, which wasn't often. Like she craved this connection the same way he did.

He was thrusting faster, deeper, lost in her, and she moaned, louder this time but still restrained, her mouth falling open as she tilted her chin up, clawing at his lower back with her fingertips. Elias felt her getting hotter, wetter around him, and he raised up on one arm, keeping his other hand buried in her hair, accelerating his movements as he met Ava's eyes again, breathing hotly against her lips.

Their mouths were touching, but they weren't kissing, only breathing one another's steamy air now, and he felt the hitch in her breath, the spike in her hip movement, the way she constricted her inner muscles around him in dizzying pleasure as she grabbed his back. Their moans were stifled only because their mouths were still pressed together, Ava swallowing the sounds that left his mouth, and he hers.

She squeezed her eyes shut, and breathed his name, and then the Creator's name, incoherently, causing chill bumps to break out over his arms. Ava was coming in forcible waves, and Elias finally allowed himself to let go too, driving into her wet warmth again, and again, and again, until his body stiffened and he came so hard, he literally saw nothing, except white light.

Even before he came down, he knew this one time wouldn't be enough with Ava. He lifted his head from the crook of her neck, and looked into her sleepy, sated eyes, still pulsing deep inside of her. Her lips parted as she drew in his air.

Elias covered the sound with another kiss.

NINE

Elias watched, eyes half-closed, as Ava crept back into the bedroom, quietly shutting the door that led to the Jack and Jill bathroom that separated his old room from Matthew's. The tiny Christmas tree was still glowing on the dresser, and he saw she was using it to help guide her way back to the bed, still unfamiliar with her surroundings.

She slipped into the sheets soundlessly, with her back facing him, probably thinking he was still asleep since it had to be close to four in the morning. It'd been a couple of hours since they both drifted off, spent and sated, Ava dozing first, her head resting on his arm, with him just a few minutes after that.

"You good?" he asked, rolling over onto his back.

She jumped a little at the sound of his quiet, groggy voice, and turned to face him, nodding her head as she tucked a hand beneath her cheek.

He smiled when she met his eyes, and so did she. Hers was soft, nearly shy, but unreserved. Her gaze drifted toward the window, where the sky was black and silent now that it'd stopped snowing.

He could practically see the thoughts milling around her brain when she blinked sleepily.

So pretty.

She smiled suddenly, raising her brows. "You know your mom has a Santa Claus in the bathroom?" Her voice was barely above a whisper. "It scared the crap out of me a second ago. It was sitting on the back of the toilet, just staring at me, like 'Ho, ho, ho, Ava.'"

He laughed quietly. "Did you speak back?"

She rolled her eyes and grinned.

"But for real," she whispered, "why does it look like—"

"Fidel Castro," they said together. Elias chuckled as Ava dissolved into soft laughter that she covered with her hand.

"I thought I was tripping!" she laughed.

"I don't know what's up with that," he said quietly, shaking his head, still grinning, when her laughter died down a bit.

"I wanna go there."

"Cuba?"

She nodded. "Havana is on my bucket list. I wanna go meet Assata Shakur."

"You'd love it," he said, keeping his voice low, watching as her eyes widened with interest.

"When'd you go?"

"Earlier this year. One of my boys did his bachelor weekend out there, so me and Jeremiah went."

"You did the Afro-Cuban tours and all that?"

"Yep. We were only there for about three days, so I didn't get to do as much as I wanted. I wanted to pop over to Varadero."

Ava shifted in the sheets, smiling. "I want to do a week there. Three days in Havana, three days at the beach."

"I said I'm gonna go back soon. You should come."

Ava raised her brows and grinned, as surprised as he was that he just blurted out the invitation like that. But, the ill part was that he realized he meant it.

For a while, they just stared at each other. Silently processing the connection between them. Like he could breathe easy with this woman. Ava blinked her eyes closed, her long eyelashes nearly brushing her cheek bones. Then she opened them again, as if she wanted to look at him too.

Elias reached out, reaching for the bottom hem of her t-shirt—his t-shirt, which she'd thrown on when she used the bathroom—urging her to slowly slide against the warm sheets, closer to him. She pressed her forehead against his shoulder then tilted her head up to press her lips to his.

He kissed her slowly. Because he didn't get enough of her the first time. Removed his t-shirt from her body slowly.

She sighed, pressing closer still, sliding her soft thighs between his before he rolled on top of her. This time, he entered her inch by inch, watching her eyes darken, chin tilt upward, lips part, before she closed her eyes, her breaths heavy yet soft.

He didn't begin moving immediately. Instead, they only kissed, his fingers buried in her curly hair. When he did start moving, it was languidly, with Ava pressing her hips up to meet his lazy strokes, breathing against his lips.

And when they did finally rest, it was with Ava, in his arms.

TEN

Natural sunlight, along with smells of bacon, fresh bread, and cinnamon, wafted from the kitchen when Ava entered from the back hallway, where the bedrooms were located.

For a long second, she hovered unseen at the entrance, taking in the early Christmas morning sounds of Elias' family. "My Favorite Things"— the Luther Vandross version. Deep, relaxed voices. Pots clanging. Light, feminine laughter.

Ava closed her eyes and took a deep breath, catching the scent of freshly brewed coffee, picking at her top lip with her thumb and index finger, before dropping her hand and rounding the corner.

At first, her presence wasn't noticed as she surveyed in the scene. Matthew was leaning against the sink counter, holding a forest green coffee mug, talking, as either Jeremiah or Daniel— she wasn't sure which because his back was turned— fried bacon in a cast iron skillet. Hope was sitting at the island bar in a maroon v-neck sweater that hung to her thighs, a colorful mug shaped like a snowman in her hand as she watched her sons, her smile peaceful and genuine.

Elias was nowhere in sight, just as it was when she woke up alone in the queen-sized bed, spent and sated, panicked and invigorated all at once, all in the single breath she took when she blinked herself to consciousness.

There was a dent in the paisley blue and gray sheets next to her, where Elias' body once was, letting her know the past few hours hadn't been a dream. The fullness between her legs was another reminder. The tenderness of her breasts, the sensitivity on her skin where her collarbone connected to her neck because Elias kissed her there more times than she could remember last night, were all indications of how fully she'd given herself over to him.

She'd spread a hand over the empty spot, her thoughts spinning, heart thudding before she spotted a small note written on a scrap of the green reindeer wrapping paper they'd used to wrap his nieces' presents last night.

"Best. Christmas. Ever."

She'd laughed aloud, burying her face in the pillow, which smelled like him. She felt as if she were in high school all over again.

Matthew looked up now, finally spotting her hovering in the kitchen entrance way, and dropped a boyish grin on her that made both of his deep dimples appear, and Ava little less like an intruder.

"Merry Christmas," he offered, his voice early morning hoarse.

"Merry Christmas," Ava returned, thankful she sounded normal when she felt anything but. "Morning everyone, Merry Christmas."

"Oh, hey there! Merry Christmas."

Hope greeted her just as she had last night as if she had

legitimate reason to be genuinely happy to see her. Ava made her way to the kitchen island, and gave her a quick hug, inhaling her comforting cocoa butter scent, pushing down the awkwardness of being in a home other than her mother's Christmas morning. It felt intrusive, even though nothing in the Young's demeanor said her insecurities were warranted.

She'd talked to her mom first thing in the morning. Jeff's daughter was still in the hospital, but they were taking the kids to breakfast and a Christmas movie. She knew Caren wanted to press her about her time at Elias' house but that was a conversation that would definitely be saved for later. She'd also talked to Ellie, who was back at her mom's, giving her a nutshell version of last night's events because she was still processing things herself.

"Coffee?" Matthew asked now, tilting his head toward the large pot of coffee that was brewed on the counter next to him. He was comfortable in a pair of sweats that hung low on his waist and long-sleeved thermal, his curly hair contained beneath another skull cap, this one black.

Ava nodded, crossing the hardwood floor to accept a mug from him, which he blindly grabbed from the cabinet above him.

"Did you sleep well?" Hope was asking. "It gets a little cold in the back bedrooms during the winter. I hope Elias showed you where the blankets were."

Ava's nod was brisk and she kept her eyes on her mug at the mention of Elias' name, and the bed where she'd had sex with him like it was her last night on earth. Like he was her last bit of pleasure ever, and she therefore had to savor every moment, swallow every drop. She almost shivered thinking about it, and goose bumps did coat her arms as flashes of his lips, tongue, fingers, hands on her neck, her belly, her thighs, invaded her brain, clinging to her memories.

"I slept well," she replied, wetting her lips before offering Hope a smile she hoped didn't look practiced. "I didn't get cold at all. Elias showed me... where everything was."

God.

She felt Jeremiah or Daniel's eyes on her, and she glanced over at him guiltily, catching the tail end of his grin before he resumed his bacon frying. She saw his profile and realized it was Jeremiah, because his beard was a little fuller and because of the way he'd grinned at her. Daniel didn't offer smiles, of any sort, easily.

Crap. Of course, everyone in the house knew she'd slept with Elias. Well, his brothers probably did since all the bedrooms were zig-zagged along the same lengthy hallway. Thankfully, Hope and Joe's bedroom was on the opposite side of the house, so they could render themselves clueless to what went on beyond their immediate area, which Ava suspected was intentional.

Ava turned to pour her coffee, closing her eyes briefly again as the steaming liquid filled her snowflake mug. Guilt. On top of the mass of emotions that were swirling in her brain and loitering in her chest cavity this morning, she felt guilty as sin for having sex in Hope's house that way, when she was clearly a spiritual, Godly woman who probably wasn't into recently rescued strangers screwing the brains out of her son on a sanctified holiday, in her home. At the same time, nothing about what she'd shared with Elias felt frivolous. It felt like *more*.

She took a scalding sip of her coffee, nearly burning her tongue and pushed out a breath in an attempt to gather herself. She turned around facing the room once more.

"Can I do anything to help?" she asked.

"No, you cannot," Hope interceded before Matthew or Jeremiah could answer. "Christmas cooking is *all* on the men in this house."

Ava smiled amusedly. "Even breakfast?"

"Even breakfast," Matthew conceded, taking a gulp of coffee.

"Mama cooks all year, no breaks," Hope said. "The men can handle one holiday."

"Have some coffee cake," Matthew offered, bobbing his head toward the kitchen island. "E made it."

"You want bacon?" Jeremiah asked her, cutting off the stove.

"Ain't nobody messing with that swine but you and dad, man."

"She's capable of making her own food choices, *man*," Hope said, rolling her eyes good-naturedly, mimicking Matthew.

"I actually did kinda want some bacon until you called it 'swine,'" Ava teased him, grinning over the brim of her cup.

Jeremiah chuckled and Matthew frowned, dimples showing again.

"That's what's wrong with black people," he said shaking his head, lightly bumping her shoulder with his. "Gotta get off that slave food. Stop eating massa's scraps."

"You take things way too far, homie," Jeremiah smirked, taking a large bite of the bacon sandwich he'd just made, chewing exaggeratedly. Hope just laughed, picking at the coffee cake on the saucer in front of her.

"Your dad still out back messing with that turkey?" Hope asked.

"I don't know why he insisted on frying it this early,"

Jeremiah frowned, glancing toward the patio door, just off the living room. "It's only 11:30."

"I told him I did not want to start eating dinner at eight this year."

"You're not gonna let us live that down, huh?" Jeremiah asked, still chewing.

"Ever," Matthew tacked on, eyeing Hope. "It was one time, Mama, three years ago."

"And I don't want a repeat," she said, grinning at Matthew's scowl.

"What time is Zoe coming with my babies?" Hope asked, taking another bite of coffee cake.

"About an hour," Matthew answered, crossing his legs as he leaned his back against the counter, next to Ava.

"You didn't want to take your dad's truck to pick them up?"

"Zoe's being stubborn. Said she has her brother's Range Rover. I ain't tryin' to fight with her about it."

Hope hummed her disapproval. Ava sipped from her mug, wondering where Elias was, and at the same time, wishing she could avoid him so she could have more time to process what went down with them last night, just as a gush of cool air swept into the room.

A few seconds later, Joe made his way into the kitchen from the garage entrance way, followed by Daniel, and lastly, Elias, sporting his black pea coat with a ball cap turned backward on his head. *Damn. He was so fine.*

Instantly, at the sight of him, her heart leaped into her stomach, and her pulse began racing double-time. Elias spotted her, and their eyes connected. The energy that was between them hadn't changed, it was buzzing and crackling, alive with intention and memory.

"Morning. Merry Christmas," he offered, his deep voice

gruff, reminding her of the way it sounded in her ear last night.

"Merry Christmas." Ava's stomach tightened as she released a breath. His gaze skimmed over mint green mock turtleneck dress, resting at the curve of her hips before floating upward to her face. The once over was quick but thorough, and Elias' grin was relaxed, as he made his way into the kitchen.

"You're back already?" Hope questioned as Joe dropped a quick kiss on her cheek, once he'd placed the turkey pan on the stove. His sons got their build from him. He was dark chocolate and at least 6'2, with the broad shoulders of a man who worked out regularly.

"I said it wouldn't take but a minute," Joe answered his wife.

Elias shrugged out of his coat, draping it over the back of one of the empty barstools at the kitchen island, revealing a caramel tan thermal that showed off his muscular arms. He came and stood next to her, reaching above her head for a coffee mug. His scent hit her, and she swallowed more coffee in a futile attempt to drown it out.

"We tried to see about your car, but they still have the interstate blocked. Think it should be cleared in another couple hours."

Ava stared up at him, unable to hide her surprise. "Oh wow, I didn't expect for you to even try to do that, Elias."

He furrowed his brow. "Why *wouldn't* I do that?" His voice was low, so that only she could hear him.

Ava shrugged. "It's not your responsibility. I was just gonna call roadside service later. You didn't have to—"

Elias shook his head slightly, eyeing her before pouring coffee into his mug. "I don't get down like that."

"Yeah but..."

"Ava," Elias interrupted quietly, fixing his coffee with a bit of cream. "I got you, okay? Let me do that."

She blinked, biting on the inside of her lip as she studied him.

"I didn't mean to bounce on you like that this morning," he told her, looking up from his mug. His deep voice was barely a rumble. "You were knocked out though, drooling on the pillow and whatnot. Thought I better let you get your rest."

"I was *not* drooling on the pillow; stop lying."

Elias chuckled quietly. Ava felt it down to her toes.

"You put some bourbon in that coffee, young lady?" Joe asked from across the room, causing her to finally tear her gaze from Elias and turn to face him. He smiled widely when she did and Ava shook her head.

"No, sir. No bourbon before noon for me."

"Ah, it's Christmas. We're on New Orleans time in this house," Joe countered, giving his wife another kiss on the cheek, squeezing her butt when she twisted her lips at him.

"Your lips are cold."

"Then warm 'em up," he said this time pecking her lips.

Ava smiled at their adorable banter, glancing at Elias, who returned her grin.

"How were the roads?" Matthew asked as he moved to stand next to the kitchen island.

"Icy," Daniel answered, through a mouth full of cake.

"Not quite as bad as it was last night but it's still cold out and not much has melted," Elias tacked on.

Matthew frowned, pulling his phone out of his sweat pockets.

"Zoe doesn't need to drive," he said, his attention momentarily distracted by the chime of the doorbell.

He went to answer it, disappearing around the corner.

Women's voices filled the foyer, along with the sound of children's giggling and feet stomping.

Seconds later, Matthew re-entered the living room, all smiles with two little girls who looked just like him in his arms, both clad in fat winter coats, one pink, the other teal. Shortly after, a woman, who she assumed was Zoe, emerged, wearing a puffy pink snow jacket, her nose red from the cold, despite her dark caramel complexion.

"You're so stubborn. I told you I was about to come get you," Matthew told her, the annoyance in his voice tempered by concern.

"I told you I was fine, scary," she returned dismissively, waving him off.

Even from across the room, Ava could see that she was gorgeous, as was the woman's behind her. Zoe smiled, revealing dimples and hair that was swept into a full, curly ponytail, making it almost appear as if she were in high school, while the other woman, whose auburn hair was braided and hanging over one shoulder, drawing out her hazelnut complexion, laughed at something Matthew said.

Hope was already off the barstool, laughing in delight as she swept her littlest granddaughter, Brielle, onto her hip, before leaning over and kissing Noelle, who was still in Matthew's arms. Just that fast, the noise level in the house doubled. Ava smiled at the bustling, as everyone greeted each other, glancing up at Elias.

But his eyes weren't on his nieces at all or Zoe. They were on the woman with the brownish hair, and she was staring at him too. The woman looked at Ava, then back to Elias, her gaze questioning. She broke eye contact, however, when Hope greeted her with a kiss on the cheek and a long hug, even though she was still holding her youngest granddaughter. Hope asked how she'd been doing, gushing about how she hadn't seen her in too long.

Ava looked up at Elias again, shifting her weight. He met her eyes for a split second before leaning down and scooping Brielle into his arms, who'd made a mad dash over to him after her Grandma finally sat her down, squealing "Unc," in her little toddler voice.

"What's up, Bri-Bri," he said, kissing her round cheek as she wiggled around in his arms, holding out a bright green pony with orange hair for him to examine. Just then the woman made their way over to Elias.

"Hi, Elias. Merry Christmas," the woman said, her voice quiet.

"Merry Christmas," he returned.

She looked over at Ava, a small, curious smile on her pretty face.

"Ava, this is Janay—Janay, Ava," Elias said, looking at her. She couldn't read his expression because he kept it neutral but her heart was now racing double-time. She knew without asking this woman was Elias' ex. The one he shared a deep history and connection with. A bond that despite the tragedy, would always exist. She was still part of his life, part of his family's life, in a significant way, obviously.

And just like that, it felt as if all her energy had been drained, replaced by something resembled disappointment but was less prodding. Disappointment implied expectation. And after everything she'd been through in the past few months and witnessed in her life, Ava knew better than that. She had to.

Ava gathered herself quickly, putting on the same smile she used when she was at work. She had to hold it together.

"Hi, it's nice to meet you," she said, extending her hand.

Janay took it, glancing at Elias again before looking her directly in the eyes.

"Nice to meet you as well, Ava."

Janay looked up at Elias again.

"You're a friend of Daniel's or Jeremiah's?" she asked, tilting her head a little. She smiled when Brielle tapped her on the shoulder, asking for "Auntie" to look at her toy, obliging the little girl's request with an exaggerated "Ooo." Ava's stomach dipped again.

"She's a friend of mine," Elias corrected, sitting the toddler, who was wiggling to get down, back on the floor.

"Oh." Janay was terrible at hiding her expressions. Hurt was palpable in her tone, in her light brown eyes, which were wide and unnaturally bright.

"So, you two traveled together for the holiday?"

"Nah," Elias answered.

"It's a long story," Ava tacked on. Janay's smile was forced and she nodded, eyes still bright.

Elias pushed out a breath, staring in his cup before looking at Janay.

Ava's gaze bounced between her and Elias, and for the first time this morning, she felt like an intruder. Her stomach twisted and she inhaled, forcing herself to take a sip of her coffee.

"Excuse me," Ava announced after another awkward second passed, tilting her head toward the back bedrooms. "I'm gonna go make some more Christmas calls."

Elias looked at her for a beat as if he wanted to same something. But no words left his lips, and Ava realized there wasn't much to be said anyway. She turned and left the kitchen.

ELEVEN

"You knew Janay was comin?" Elias didn't look up at Matthew, as he carved the fried turkey.

Matthew gave him a "come on, man" look, replacing the lid on the gumbo.

"You know Zoe don't ever tell me shit. I thought maybe you talked to her or somethin'."

"Nah."

"It's kinda wild she just popped up. But then she's had it like that for a minute," Matthew rationalized, not looking at him as he stirred the rice cooking on the stove.

Elias glanced at Matthew but said nothing. About a month ago, Janay started calling a little more frequently. And they'd talked a little. Mostly about work, or Janay offering her opinion about Matthew and Zoe's back-and-forth, nothing major. Nothing about them. To Elias, it felt like maybe they were getting back to being cool again after the way they fell apart, which felt good. He loved Janay, even though it didn't work out, and he didn't want shit messy between them. They had too much history for that. And she was Zoe's best friend. Their parents were cool. It didn't make sense for them to be at each other's throats.

But then, things turned. She started calling a little more often, later at night. Reminiscing about the past. Suggesting they maybe hang out when he had a minute. And so, they did. Because that's what was natural for them. Falling backward. But not anymore.

That last time, Elias felt something shift in his gut. He knew that their shared history didn't have the power to outweigh the space they'd landed in now. He thought Janay was on the same page. But then last night, while he was wrapping gifts with Ava, she'd texted him, *"I miss you."* He hadn't responded.

Maybe it was bullshit, but he just didn't want the drama of explaining why it wouldn't ever work between them. He figured the holidays likely made her more emotional, but if he just stalled her out a little bit, she'd probably come to her own realization about them. But now, with her popping up over his folks' on Christmas Day, as if it was still like that with them—he was gonna have to have the conversation again. He'd muddled their relationship, allowing things to go there again with her.

He glanced up from the turkey meat, his eyes finding and landing on Ava, who was sitting on the couch in the living room. He could just make out the back of her head from over the couch. Jeremiah was running a little interference for him, keeping things cool, engaging with Ava ever since Janay arrived and Zoe started with the crazy looks. He loved Zoe like a sister but he told Matthew to check her on that shit, or he would.

"I'll get her straight, man," Matthew said, shaking his head.

It was awkward for him so he could only imagine how

Ava was feeling. They'd barely said two words to each other over the past two hours because she was actively avoiding him. They were on some high school mess for real, right now. When he tried to pull her to the back bedroom to talk, she went, reluctantly, and listened to him tell her he didn't know Janay was coming, and wasn't trying to put her in a weird position. She didn't have much to say, other than "it's fine" and "okay."

"*You didn't know I was coming, Elias,*" she said. "*This your life—I'm the one interrupting, you know?*"

"*This ain't my life, though. Janay being here like this ain't my life.*"

"Okay."

She'd met his eyes directly, but the wariness was back, or maybe not that. More like her expectation that he'd mess up was fulfilled. That he even cared about her expectations after only one night, let him know he didn't want her slipping completely out of his life. He wanted to know her.

He shook his head. They needed to have a real conversation. He *did* want to get to know her. Not scare her off with extra shit before he got a chance to do that for real. And after last night... He sliced the meat, his groin tightening just thinking about how Ava felt wrapped around him, how he just wanted to bury himself in her. She messed his head *all the way up*.

"Are we about ready?" Hope came into the kitchen, peering onto the stove.

"Yep, you can call everyone," Elias said.

"Okay," his mom nodded, peering at him before glancing toward the patio, where Janay was outside with Noelle and Zoe, who were writing their names in the light dusting of snow that covered the wood.

Hope's gaze skated to Ava, who was now laughing at

something Jeremiah said. Brielle bounced up to Ava, holding out her arms, and Ava smiled widely, pulling the wiggly little girl onto her lap.

"Oooo, no she didn't," Hope said, grinning, eyes wide, making her look at least ten years younger than sixty-two. Brielle was notoriously shady, only going to people she knew, and sometimes ignoring even them.

Ava pressed her cheek to Brielle's, widening her eyes and clapping when she pulled back, responding to whatever his toddler niece was chattering about. Jeremiah held out his arms for her and Brielle shook her head, as Ava laughed. Elias felt himself automatically smiling at the sight of it. Hope glanced up at Elias, her eyes knowing.

"Come on everyone," she called. "We need to pray."

"CAN WE TALK?"

Janay's voice was quiet when she approached, seating herself on the couch next to him. They'd just finished eating and Jeremiah, his dad and Daniel had all retreated to the den for a drink, while Zoe and Matthew disappeared somewhere, as they frequently did at family functions. Elias was fairly certain that's how Brielle was conceived, at Thanksgiving a few years ago.

Dinner was good, the awkwardness mostly overpowered by everyone being together, genuinely enjoying one another's company. Last year, the first year after Kayla's death, he and Janay had been on the verge of ending things, and the grief had been overwhelming, as he watched Noelle and especially Brielle, bouncing around the house. Kayla was just three months younger than Brielle, and Zoe and Janay had been pregnant together.

That first holiday season after her death was brutal, for the entire family. The shift this year was noticeable, though unspoken. Lighter. Easier. Even Daniel seemed to be brooding less.

Now, Elias was chilling in the living room, half watching the Lakers, but mostly watching Ava as she helped Noelle load the dishwasher, chattering with her about that show, *Angel Hunter*, which Noelle had no business watching. Elias looked at Janay, who was waiting for him to respond to her soft request. He bit the inside of his lip and released it, finally pushing up from the couch.

"Out there?" Janay bobbed her head toward the patio door and he nodded again, knowing he needed to get the conversation over with. He glanced in Ava's direction once more. Her eyes were on him now, where they stayed until he finally slipped out the door into the cold, Janay on his heels.

"I know this is weird," Janay started, her nose already turning red in the cold. She was fair skinned, with a complexion the color of butterscotch, and eyes that weren't much darker than her skin, holding hints of green as well.

"I shouldn't have just come here without calling."

She stuffed her hands into her sweater pockets, looking up at him, almost as if she wanted him to dispute her assertion. She was short, no more than 5'2, and first, that'd been a turn on. He liked feeling as if Janay needed his protection. Later, he wondered if maybe she didn't need it *too* much. And if maybe he didn't like that because he had some things he needed to work out too. Janay looked out over the perfectly manicured back yard when he didn't respond, shaking her head.

"I just wanted to see you," she said softly. "Talking to you again lately, has been... refreshing. And this is my parent's cruise year and I wasn't feeling it at all, so I thought I'd come by."

She stopped and blew out a breath. "I meant what I said last night, Elias. I've been thinking about you— about *us* a lot lately. Have you? Been thinking about us?"

He sighed, watching his breath fog in the cold.

"Of course, I think about you, Janay." He met her eyes. "I hope you're good. I pray things are working out for you. That you're getting what you want."

"Yeah, but do you think about *me*, still?"

Her gaze was unwavering. So much history. So many moments, ups and downs, all gathered in her hazel eyes.

"I think about you."

She smiled a little and he shook his head.

"But we moved on, Janay. We both moved on because that other shit we were on? It was toxic for us both."

"Did we move on though? We were just together two weeks ago, Elias."

Elias looked out over the yard.

"That felt real. That didn't feel like that past."

"Didn't it though?" he countered, his gaze back on her. "What happened afterward didn't feel like that past to you, Janay?"

Janay shook her head. "It doesn't have to be that way now."

"It *is* that way. That last time—it was like, a wake-up call. We don't work like that any more."

"We were both in so much pain after Kayla..."

"It was never just about Kayla. The way things went so far left with us was never only about Kayla."

He stared at her, and she blinked looking down at the ground.

"Do you still think about her?"

His brow furrowed immediately. *What kind of shit—*

"Every day. She was my daughter, Janay."

He felt old pricks of the anger and resentment in his chest. That was Janay's go-to in the end. His silence meant he didn't really care. About her. About their loss. About anything.

"I still love you," Janay said now.

She looked up at him.

He sighed. "I love you too."

"I'm *in* love with you, Elias."

Last year, even six months ago, Janay's admission would've been enough for him to try again. But after that slip-up a couple weeks ago, it was clear to him the space between them, the emotional distance, was oceans wide now. Having the space to breathe, without the emotional baggage they'd carried between them for so long, was freeing.

"We can't keep doing this. It's not good for us. We've done this so many times."

Back and forth. Make up to break up. Both of them separating for a time only to come back together because it was easier than being alone and dealing, easy to fall back into a cycle of familiarity, even after the desire to be there had left, replaced with obligation.

"Are you dating her?"

Her cheeks were pink and she wet her lips, her gaze questioning, nearly accusatory.

"We're getting to know each other."

"Zoe said you just met last night."

Elias rolled his eyes. "Zoe needs to mind her business."

"She's just looking out for me."

If she was looking out for you, you wouldn't be here. But

he didn't say it aloud. Janay pressed her lips together, as if she wanted to say more but was suppressing it.

"Did you sleep with her?"

He stared at her, cocking his head, brows raised. She huffed out a breath and looked away.

"That's irrelevant anyway," she said, finally. "This is about me and you. I know we've been doing our own thing but... we have a lot of history. That doesn't just disappear. It means something. And after what happened the other week..."

He stuffed his hands into his pockets, shaking his head. "That wasn't... We gotta leave it there, Janay. You know we do."

She frowned and looked away.

"C'mon let's go inside. It's cold out here."

"Exactly." She glared at him, her mood changed, just that fast.

"Exactly what?"

"Exactly what you always do, Elias. Run. Leave when things get inconvenient."

He pushed out a breath and shook his head.

"I'm going inside."

"Why?"

"Because I'm not tryin' to sit out here in the freezing cold with you, arguing the same argument we've been having for forever."

She rolled her eyes, tears welling in them again.

He sighed. "Why don't you come back inside?"

"You can go back in. I'm good out here."

He shook his head, pulling open the patio door, just in time to hear the front door close on the opposite end of the house.

Immediately, he looked toward the kitchen. No Ava. *Shit.*

"Hey, Noelle, where'd Ava go?" he asked his niece as she skipped past him toward the den, her eyes on whatever device she'd received for Christmas.

"She's outside with that man," she answered, dismissively.

With that man? Elias grabbed his coat from off the back of the bar chair just as Janay walked back into the house, watching him. He couldn't say he didn't care about the look on her face but he couldn't dwell on it either, as he quickly rounded the corner, headed for the front door.

Ava looked up at the sound of the front door of the house closing, then turned back to the tow truck driver, who has just finished unloading her car across the street from the house.

"You were just gonna leave without sayin' anything?" he asked, when he reached her, his breath puffing in the cold. He was trying to keep his tone even but what the hell?

"I called to see if I could get someone out to get my car before dinner since I got a text saying the roads were clear," she explained. "I came back in to thank you again for all of your help but I didn't want to interrupt you."

The look in her eyes told him she'd heard at least a little of his conversation with Janay. Probably the part about them being together a couple weeks ago, if he had to guess from her expression.

She turned and accepted the slip from the lanky, mustached man. He shook his head and took it from her, ignoring her when she started to object. He pulled out his wallet so he could pay the dude.

Elias looked at her while his card was being run, but she looked away, off down the icy street, her lips in a tight line.

"Thanks, man. Appreciate it," Elias said, nodding at the guy, who saluted him after handing his card back.

"Thank you," Ava told the guy, earning her a salute as well.

"Thank you but you didn't need to do that," she told him.

He ignored her.

"So, what's up?" he asked. "You're just gonna drive back to Atlanta right now?"

"I want to leave before it gets dark. I'm gonna stop and get gas first, so you don't have to worry about fetching me from the side of the road again." She offered him a plastic smile, and Elias frowned.

"Why are you just leaving like this?"

"It's time for me to go," she said pointedly. "I wasn't supposed to be here in the first place."

"Come on, Ava."

"Come on, what?" Her eyes were lowered when she looked at him, nostrils slightly flared. "So, I *was* supposed to be here, spending Christmas with your family and your ex?"

"I didn't know she was coming."

"I know," Ava said, resignedly, staring down at her brown boots. "It doesn't matter like that anyway. We had our night. It's over. We should just... go our separate ways."

"I ain't tryin' to do that."

"Well, I am."

He stepped closer to her, and her back hit the side of her door. He saw her intake of breath.

"That isn't what it felt like last night."

He stared into her midnight eyes, challenging her to remember. He could see by the way her pupils dilated that she did.

"Last night was last night," she retorted. "We should leave it there."

He shook his head, stepping closer still, so that they were touching. He grabbed the bottom hem of her leather jacket, tugging her slightly toward him. She wet her lips when he stared down at them.

"You need to handle your stuff, Elias. Because what's going on in there," she tilted her head toward the house, "I've been there, done that. And I'm not trying to go there with you. I don't normally... I've never done anything like this before. And now I know why because this isn't me, and it's not how I want to feel."

The vulnerability in her eyes overpowered her anger.

He put his hands in her coat pockets, pulling her against him, as he released a breath.

"I hear you. I do. I ain't about drama either. It caught me off guard today. But that," he bobbed his head toward the house too, "that ain't where my head's at."

"You're still in love with her."

"No," he said immediately because it was true. "I haven't been for a while."

"Are you over her?"

"Yes," he answered because that was true too.

She blinked up at him, and he could tell she was trying not to press against his body because when they were this close to each other, it was difficult not to touch.

"When we get back to Atlanta, I'll call you. And the invite to New Year's Eve still stands. I really wanna see you again before that."

She blew out a cold breath and looked away. He pulled her closer, with his hands still in her coat pocket.

"Ava."

She looked up at him.

"I wanna see you again."

She bit her lip and he pulled her against him again.

"Can I see you again?"

He could see the debate in her eyes when she looked into his. Finally, she blinked and looked away.

"I need to go," she breathed, refusing to meet his eyes.

For a long second he didn't move. She was staring off down the street and he was staring at her. When it was obvious she wasn't going to relent, he sighed, reluctantly taking a step backward.

Immediately, Ava opened the car door, sliding into the driver's seat.

"Can you let me know you got back safely?" he asked before she shut the door.

She looked at him and nodded, and he knew she was lying. He backed away from her car, stuffing his hands in his pockets. Ava looked up at him once then drove away.

TWELVE

"We should go."

Ava ignored Ellie as they made their way through the crowd gathered at Ponce City Market, people who also decided today would be a great one to get out, because after falling below freezing just a few days prior, it was now hovering around sixty degrees.

It always seemed to Ava that people had an extra pep in their step right before the New Year. All Ava wanted was the Barolo she loved, at Ponce City Market had the only wine store in Atlanta that sold it.

"We oughta just pop up over there tonight after church," Ellie persisted as they dipped into the moderately crowded wine bar and store. "You'd mess his head up."

Ava rolled her eyes. "I'm not trying to mess up anybody's head."

"Well, he definitely messed *yours* up," Ellie retorted, arching a brow as they wandered over to the Italian section of the wine.

"Nobody messed my head up," Ava lied.

"I can't believe you actually slept with him," Ellie said,

studying the wines. She looked up at Ava. "My mind is still blown."

Just the mention of Elias made her heart race, along with her thoughts. Just the reminder of him was enough to distract her, send her into a daydreaming tailspin. She hadn't seen him in a week since she left his parents' house on Christmas Day. Hadn't talked to him either. Not once. He called, and every time he did, she ignored it, even though it was hard. Everything she heard and witnessed on Christmas told Ava that no matter what he believed, Elias wasn't available to her. But that didn't keep her from wishing. Imaging a scenario where neither one of them had any significant baggage, and they could really see what they could be.

"Well, I wanna see what's up with Kendrick," Ellie said.

"Then you should see what's up with Kendrick," Ava said absently, scanning the massive wine section.

That was the thing about coming into Wine Down, she always ended up getting sidetracked. She grabbed the red blend she'd been staring at, and continued down the aisle to where her Barolo was typically located.

"I want you to come with me, though, in case the vibe isn't right," Ellie practically whined.

"And mess up *my* vibe?"

Ellie paused mid-aisle when Ava did.

"And why would the vibe be messed up?" Ava questioned. "I thought you two were on the same page."

"We are. But you know men are trash. It's a new day. He might start acting brand new."

Ava smirked.

"You know you want to see Elias." Ellie wiggled her brows.

Ava bit the inside of her lip, staring unseeingly at wine bottles. Of course, she wanted to see him.

"He's drama. And I don't need that."

She thought of Elias outside on the porch with Janay, her reminding him that they'd been together as early as two weeks ago. They obviously had a back-and-forth relationship that Ava wanted no parts of, even though it hurt. Way more than it should've.

"He literally told you he wants to get to know you. And that he's not with ol' girl anymore and he's over her. You know I wouldn't be sticking up for a shady character but the way you talked about him, and the way he's been blowing up your phone... I dunno, Ava. Don't let Ty ruin you," Ellie said as Ava finally selected her wine. At that, Ava looked up at her.

"Ruin me?"

"Yes," Ellie said, her eyes serious. "Well, not *ruin* you but," she shrugged. "Change you. Make you all afraid and suspicious. Scared to give anybody a legit chance."

"Um, aren't you the person who literally said, 'all men are trash,' like five seconds ago?"

"Don't give him power he shouldn't have," Ellie warned again, ignoring her, sounding just like her mother.

Ty had been blowing up her phone for the past week and she finally answered because she was starting to think something was wrong. It was a mistake because Ty didn't want anything important at all, only to chit-chat, as if he still had the option to do that with her.

After that, she'd stopped answering his calls too. She was done being concerned with men period. She was going back to work in another week and she'd turn her focus that way. Maybe realistically start plotting her exit from the network and the launch of her company.

"*Yo,*" Ellie suddenly uttered under her breath, eyes wide. She subtly nodded her head in the direction of the South African section on the next aisle over. "It's fate."

Ava followed her gaze, her pulse racing rapidly the second she spotted him.

"*Crap.*"

Ava turned, ready to make a break for it. Ellie rolled her eyes.

"He's *one* aisle over, dude. He's gonna see you if you go running out of the store like Usain Bolt, Ava," Ellie chastised quietly.

"Crap," she muttered again.

"Be cool; he's coming over here," Ellie said under breath. "You okay?"

Ava nodded quickly, and inhaled, turning back around, her eyes fixed on the wine display.

"Ava."

She looked up at the sound of Elias' sexy baritone, and tried to feign surprise. He smirked, and she knew he wasn't buying it.

"Hey Elias."

He grinned and she couldn't help but smile back. He looked good. Better than good. A black pea coat covered his shoulders, his jeans low on his hips, the burnt orange sweater he was wearing bringing out the rich chocolate tone of his skin. And glasses. He was wearing glasses, which gave him an entirely new level of sexy.

"I didn't know you wore glasses," she said lamely.

He grinned, giving her another look that said he thought she was adorable. "Just when my contacts are bothering me."

He quickly exchanged greetings with Ellie but even then, barely took his eyes off her.

"So, you're wine shopping?" she asked the obvious, her gaze dropping to the bottle in his hand, a South African pinotage she'd never heard of before.

"Had to grab some for tonight." His eyes skated over her features, as if soaking her up, and heat spread throughout her body. A week hadn't killed her pull to him. Not even close.

"How've you been?" he asked, his voice dipping an octave. It didn't sound like a nicety coming from him but like he really was concerned with her wellbeing.

"I've been good. Just laying low, chilling out mostly."

She could tell he wanted to ask about her ignoring his calls, but instead chewed on the inside of his bottom lip, his gaze penetrating once more.

Ellie had casually wandered off toward the opposite end of the store, giving them space. Ava pushed out a breath.

"Come have a drink with me," he offered, just as she was about to tell him goodbye.

"I can't."

"The bar's right there." He bobbed his head toward the right of the space, where there was a bar running alongside the wall, with metallic stools. "Just one drink, Ava."

"I can't. We have a few more stops to make."

"And then?" he stepped a little closer, bringing his warm masculine scent with him.

"I'm going to the eight o'clock watch service at Ellie's church."

"Then come by when you're finished."

"I can't."

"You stay fighting me, Ava," he said exasperatedly, his voice low and somehow intimate, even in this very public, busy space. "What's up with that?"

"I'm not fighting you, Elias."

He released a breath, eyes never leaving hers.

"The invitation still stands," he said, reading the stubbornness in hers, "whenever you're ready." She swallowed, looking down at her feet before raising her gaze to his. *Move away, Ava.*

"Bye Elias."

She turned and went to find Ellie.

THIRTEEN

He felt like a stalker.

For the second time tonight, Elias was on Ava's page, scrolling. He wasn't even really looking for shit. Seeing her today, so unexpectedly, reintroduced the craving he'd had for her since she left him a week ago. After one night of kicking it. It didn't make any sense that night, and a week later, it still didn't.

It wasn't just that she was effortlessly pretty, or that his attraction to her was so magnetic. It was her entire vibe that made him want to be near her, just get a little bit more of her energy.

But after his fifth phone call after Christmas he decided to chill. She obviously wasn't feeling it, and if she was, she was too skeptical to act on whatever it was between them.

He couldn't fault her for being on guard because of Janay. He'd gone back inside after Ava peeled off on Christmas and Janay was waiting for him, ready to pick a fight. He was irritated but he also felt bad for her because he was sure her tripping wasn't about him, or them, at all. She was missing something and was reaching for what was familiar to fill it. He knew, he'd been there with her too many times before. They didn't talk again before she left with Zoe later that evening and he hadn't spoken to Janay since, opting to ignore her call the couple of times she contacted him.

He was really finished this time. And she needed the space to realize he was firm in his decision.

His gaze landed on Ava's pretty face again, smiling up from his phone screen, before he clicked out of her page, running a hand over his head. He grabbed his whiskey up off the end table, refocusing on the conversation he'd been drifting in and out of with Kendrick and Jeremiah's friend, Lashay, and her girl whose name he didn't catch. Well, "friend" might've been a generous description for Lashay. He got up, heading toward the kitchen, bored with the conversation, making his way past a group of folks Jeremiah invited.

His house was full but not so crowded he wasn't always aware of what was going on, which is the way he liked to keep their New Year's Eve parties. A couple years ago, before mass gentrification and skyrocketing prices, he'd bought the small, three-bedroom split-level, located just around the corner from the Atlanta University Center. Back then folks looked at him like he was crazy for living in the so-called hood. But he'd never been about that—scared of his own people. Aware, sure. Scared? Hell nah. It was a new craftsman style house, built to look older, with hardwood throughout and a compact space that was airy because there were few walls. Right now, A Tribe Called Quest was playing, echoing through the living room and kitchen, as people bobbed their head to the mellow bass groove of "Find My Way."

"Who's that with Lashay?" Daniel asked, when he

entered the kitchen, where the makeshift bar was located. He poured a bit of whiskey in his plastic red cup before grabbing a chicken wing.

Elias shrugged, munching on his wing. "Ja-something I think. You check out that lead Kendrick sent you?"

Daniel was contemplating moving from Dallas to Atlanta, especially since he was divorced now and had no real reason to stay in Texas when the family was in Georgia. His ex wife's people were Texas natives, and Daniel made the adjustment. But now it was time for him to come home. Kendrick was trying to find him a reasonably priced spot, somewhere in town.

"Tomorrow," Daniel answered.

The woman Daniel had been checking out, Lashay's friend, got up, heading toward the kitchen. Daniel's expression didn't change much, but his eyes did run the length of her. She was Daniel's type. Skin the color of dark coffee and petite, with a big chest. The woman came into the kitchen and poured herself a drink, chatting with them idly, though it was clear she was interested in Daniel, who'd leaned against the counter and was openly assessing her, a half-grin on his face.

Elias dropped his attention to his phone again, which was buzzing, his gaze falling on Ava's face again. Apparently, he hadn't clicked out of her page after all. And again, just from looking at her picture, that irrational pull in the center of his chest activated like a trip alarm.

Even at the wine bar earlier, it took everything in him not to touch her. Not to *beg* her, just to give him a minute. To chill with whatever thoughts were racing through her busy head, and get to know him. She'd been rocking a pair of those stretchy blue jeans, the kind that made women with no ass look like they had one. But Ava didn't need the jeans because she did. And the cut of her jacket made it even more noticeable. Her black leather jacket was unzipped to just above her cleavage and it almost looked as if she wasn't wearing anything beneath it, until she turned and he got a glimpse of her blue shirt poking from beneath.

Elias squinted as his phone, then stuffed it back in his pocket.

"I'm gonna make a run right quick," he told Daniel, who was engaged in a pretty one-sided conversation with ol' girl.

"Don't let anybody tear up my shit."

"Where you headed? It's ten forty-five."

"To handle something."

Daniel eyed him. "Alright," he said, smirking.

Now that he'd made the decision to bounce, he couldn't get out of the house fast enough, ducking and dodging nosy folks and Matthew's questioning eyes as he slid out of his house.

Thirty minutes later, he was walking up the worn sidewalk to a small bungalow on the west side. He rapped on the door then stuffed his hands back into his pockets because the temperature had dropped significantly since this morning.

Ava didn't even look surprised to see him when she opened the door.

FOURTEEN

"What's up, Elias?"

Ava bit the inside of her lip, eyeing him warily as he hovered outside on her porch. He knew without question Ellie called her friend as soon as he finished wrangling Ava's address from her, so, she knew he was coming.

"Ellie gave me your address," he told her anyway.

She twisted her lips and nodded, her midnight eyes still trained on him. Finally, she released a breath and stepped aside, allowing him to enter.

He leaned against the back of the door, only mildly aware of his surroundings, vaguely noting her place smelled like vanilla, and was decorated in warm pastels—peaches, browns, and soft blues. Instead, he focused on Ava. She was comfortable in a pair of leggings and a long Mavericks t-shirt, with a pair of fuzzy socks on her feet, glass of red wine in her hand. It was bold, maybe even stupid, popping up when he wasn't sure if she was entertaining some dude but he needed to see her.

"How was church?" he asked, when she crossed an arm over her middle, holding her wine with the other hand.

"You came over here to ask me about church?"

"I came over here because I wanted to see you."

She released a breath.

"Church was good. I made a list of affirmations and goals."

"Oh yeah?"

She nodded. "To be honest with myself. To be honest with other people. And to get paid."

She smiled when she said that last part and he chuckled. Ava looked down at her feet before meeting his eyes again.

"I thought you were having a New Year's Eve party."

"I am."

"And you left your party to come here?"

"I wanted to see you," he said again.

"Elias..."

"Ava. Come with me."

"To the party?"

"Yeah. I want you there."

She twisted her lips and smiled, staring at the ground again.

"Please?"

He was begging.

She lifted her gaze to his. "Okay," she said finally. "But only as part of my affirmation this year, to be honest with myself."

She shifted her weight, then met his eyes. "I wanna spend some time with you too, Elias."

He smiled, and she did too.

"Give me a second to get dressed."

THEY MADE it back to his place just in time for the countdown. He had her trapped between his arms as she leaned against her back against his patio railing. He'd pulled her outside when they first arrived, away from the noise, and Ellie, who showed up as well, wanting to be alone with her. She seemed to be on the same page, snuggling close to his chest, stuffing her hands in his coat pockets. He looked down at her and grinned.

"Best. New Year's Eve. Ever."

He chuckled, dodging her light swat at his shoulder, when she murmured how corny he was, laughing. Inside they were counting down. Ava looked up at him, her eyes the color of the night sky, warm and open. He brushed his nose against hers, and she inhaled his air.

"Happy New Year, Elias," she whispered.

He smiled and pressed his lips to hers.

READ an excerpt from the second part of Ava and Elias' story, *The Morning After*, coming soon!

CHAPTER 1

Ava opened an eyelid, drawing in a long slow breath as her brain slowly came awake. It wasn't quite there yet. She arched her back a little as she stretched, snuggling back into the warm blanket, blinking sleepily in an attempt to clear her foggy vision. It was still dark outside, indicating the early hour.

Her gaze landed on the solid arm draped around her middle, and her heart picked up pace, as it had for the past three mornings, when she woke up with her limbs wrapped in Elias Young's, her butt pressed against his morning erection.

She shifted against him and he automatically drew her closer, even though his chest was still moving evenly, signaling that he wasn't even awake yet. She closed her eyes again, picking absently at her bottom lip.

The fact that she was awaking in his bed for the third morning in a row, was doing too much. Way, way too much.

She'd came over late for his annual New Year's Eve party, and hadn't left yet. He'd asked her to stay that night, as they rang in the new year in the cold night air, standing on the back of his wooden patio, and she'd tried to resist, at first. But then he'd quietly said her name in his way that was a caress with a hint of demand—*"Ava"*— and her reservations fell away like her clothes later did that night. *"Stay the night with me,"* he'd asked, his voice low in her ear, making her entire body heat, in spite of the winter night air.

"Okay." Her breath puffed in the cold as she acquiesced and Elias pulled her tighter against his body, dropping slow, warm kisses into the side of her neck, until they were interrupted by his older brother, Daniel, who wanted to know where the extra supply of bourbon was.

After that, they'd gone inside and hung out with everyone, though Elias never drifted far from her side. He refreshed her wine. He made sure she ate, and much later, when the house was quiet and empty, he'd taken care of her every physical desire, pleasing her before she even formed a full idea of what she wanted, where she wanted him to touch her.

New Year's Day had been no different. She'd lounged around the house with him, nosing in the kitchen as he made ribs, sautéed spinach and black-eyed peas with cornbread, and he told her to stay for dinner. Dinner turned to breakfast. And the next day, yesterday, they'd watched the entire first season of *Game of Thrones*, her for the second time, him for the first because he wanted to see what the hype was about—even though he was years late.

When she'd made a move to leave late that evening—which was admittedly half-hearted, he told her he'd just ordered a pizza and poured her another glass of a delicious South African red blend. Wine turned to night, which turned to this morning.

"Winter is coming."

Elias sleepy baritone broke her out of her thoughts and Ava laughed, her shoulders shaking with the movement.

"I dreamt about Khaleesi," Ava admitted, turning her head to look at him.

"Me too. I dreamt I bought you some dragon eggs at an auction, and you were mad because I put I didn't put them in the refrigerator."

Ava laughed again as Elias chuckled.

"That's why I don't binge watch late at night," she said. "I always wind up dreaming about the show."

His answer was to kiss her shoulder, sending goosebumps dancing down the length of her arm at the feel of his scratch hair on her warm skin.

"What do you have going on today?" she asked, turning onto her back to look up at him.

He grinned when their eyes met, and she automatically smiled too. Elias was *sexy*. And fine. And chill. And she felt comfortable with him in a way that made absolutely no sense, which is why trepidation lingered deep in her belly. She raised her brows, still smiling when he didn't answer.

"What?" she asked, because of the way he was looking at her.

"I like you."

Her body heated and she rolled her eyes smiling. "I like you too... obviously. I haven't seen my home in three days."

"My bad," he said, not looking sorry at all, a half-grin on his face. "Had you hemmed up over here, huh?"

She smiled. "I'm not complaining. Just.. you know."

She lifted a shoulder, shifting her weight, feeling like a school girl under Elias' steady gaze. He was giving her that look again, the one that turned her into mush, made her body come alive and thrum in anticipation.

"You never answered," she prompted, when he grinned again, fully aware of how she instantly reacted to him.

"I just picked up a gig with Ford, so I gotta fly out to L.A. today."

Her eyes widened and she attempted to sit up. "Oh, I can g—"

"Uh-uh, uh-uh," Elias furrowed his brow, shaking his head, his grin still in place. "Whatchu doin?"

He brushed his nose against her collarbone, planting a kiss into the side of her neck.

"You just said you have a flight," Ava said, her eyes automatically drifting closed at the feel of Elias' lips pressed against her skin. His large hand trailed to her hip, palming it as he kissed the underside of her neck.

"I ain't leavin *now*," he said, a hint of amusement in his baritone. "Not til later this afternoon."

"How long will you be gone?"

"Not sure," he said against her neck, resting his head on

his outstretched arm. Somehow her leg was between his and he ran his hand up ribcage back down to her hip.

"About three, four days, probably. Maybe a week."

"L.A. is a cool town," Ava said, nodding, wondering if she sounded as lame to him as she felt. "Do you go there a lot for business?"

"Lately. For about the past year, now that I'm getting bigger contracts."

"Oh, cool. That's really cool, and good that you're getting the work."

She bit the inside of her cheek hard to keep the word "cool" from leaving her lips again. Why the hell was she so goofy all of a sudden? Her stomach was now knotted and she drew in a silent breath as realization hit her—she didn't want him to leave. She wanted to stay all up under this man, and have him all up under her. After three days. She was tripping. Hard. They were silent for a moment, their bodies growing warm from being pressed together under the blankets. She could feel his chest rising and falling with his breaths, as he traced her skin with his fingertips. The air between them had shifted.

"Ava, can I be real?" Elias asked after a minute.

He lifted his head and looked at her.

"I miss you already."

She blinked, drawing in a breath.

"Shit's crazy, right?" He raised a brow, a whisper of a smile on his handsome face, when he met her eyes.

"I—" she stopped and closed her mouth. "Me too," she admitted.

Because that's what she did with Elias, apparently. Told her whole truth, with very little prompting. He grinned a little at her acknowledgement.

"So, I'll call you," he said, his voice still sleepy sexy. "And when I get back, I'll see you."

It wasn't a suggestion and Ava smiled.

"Cool," she agreed, tilting her head up to receive his kiss as he smiled and rolled on top of her.

Her legs fell open, her body already warm and ready for him. They'd done this for the past three mornings, made love in the early morning dark, coming together in a string of soft sighs and moans as the sun rose beyond Elias' bedroom window.

Elias reached between them, running two fingers along the length of her, biting his lip and making a small sound from deep in his chest when he found her already wet. He positioned himself to enter her, quietly groaning his pleasure as he slowly entered her, sending shivers over her skin as he looked her in the eyes. Those first few seconds when Elias pushed his way into her felt so delicious, she never wanted the sensation to end. She drew in a sharp breath, her lips parting, eyes closing at how damn *good* he felt.

"Good morning," he said low in her ear, pressing into her further, causing her to arch her back, her fingers digging into the small of his back. She smiled as he brushed his nose against hers, setting a lazy, sensual rhythm. He smiled too when she ran her hands up his muscled back, and wrapped her arms around his neck.

"Good morning."

AFTERWORD

I love the holiday season. The smells, the music, the vibe, the lights, the decorations, the love. The *Charlie Brown Christmas* soundtrack is literally playing in my house as I type this.

Anyway, this novella started out as a holiday super-short that I wrote about two years ago—*The Christmas Party*. Basically, it was Elias and Ava's meet-cute and many of you said you wanted to read more about this couple. Two years later... here we are.

I really wrote this novella for y'all, and ended up falling in love with this couple. That said, I truly hope you enjoyed it.

Until Next Time,
Love & Peace,
Jacinta

ACKNOWLEDGMENTS

Thank you to my mom. As always, I appreciate you beyond words. You read. You correct. You daydream. You encourage. You're the best mom ever.

To the awesome Lily Java, who has totally saved me with my last two releases, THANK YOU. To Nia Forrester, who is truly, constantly one of my biggest inspirations, thank you. And to Rae Lamar, whose encouragement is so appreciated, thank you. I'm so grateful for y'all.

To all of the readers who've rocked with me from day one, and to those who may've just started reading my books, thank you. I strive to be better, for you.

I'm grateful to the Lord Jesus for the ability to do what I love. Sweet.

KEEP UP WITH MY RELEASES!

Click to Join My Mailing List!

Join my newsletter to get updates on new releases, upcoming projects, sales, teasers, snippets, exclusive giveaways, and other cool whatnots.

ALSO BY JACINTA HOWARD

The Prototype Series

Happiness In Jersey

Finding Kennedy

Keeping Willow

Loving Cassie

The Prototype 'Glimpse' Series: Short Stories From The Prototype

The Love Below

The Love Always Series

Better Than Okay

More Than Always

Less Than Forever

The Young Brothers Series

The Night Before

The Morning After (Coming Soon)

Standalone Titles

Blind Expectations

Always (A Blind Expectations Novellete)

ABOUT THE AUTHOR

Jacinta Howard is an Atlanta-based culture and entertainment journalist and contemporary romance author. She digs summertime and flip flops, deep bass lines and good lyrics, goofy jokes, and kind people. A *USA Today* 'Must Read' author, she believes there's an Andre 3000 lyric to fit any situation.

Love is beautiful. Humans are messy.
I write about the space in between.

Jacintahoward.net

Made in the USA
Columbia, SC
29 June 2023